MW00782104

Lipstick & Danger

A COLLECTION OF SHORT STORIES
WHEN ESCAPE IS YOUR ONLY OPTION

AWARD-WINNING AUTHOR
TIERNEY JAMES

Publishing Coordinator – Sharon Kizziah-Holmes
Cover Design – Jaycee DeLorenzo

Paperback-Press
an imprint of A & S Publishing
A & S Holmes, Inc.

ISBN -13: 978-1-956806-51-9

DEDICATION

To Gwen Guymon Roberts
who is not only a fan but a dear friend. Thanks for
all your encouragement. If you hadn't
suggested I start this project I might never have
tried it.

ACKNOWLEDGMENTS

Paperback Press & Sharon Kizziah-Holmes: You never give up on me and push me to do better. You are loved and appreciated.

Shirley McCann: Thanks for putting on your editor hat for this little book. You continue to amaze me in everything you do.

Lipstick & Danger Reader Group: https://www.facebook.com/groups/2430789897157949 Every day you show up to make me laugh at your comments. You are a creative bunch who bring fun and thought-provoking ideas to the mix. Thank you for coming along on this wonderful journey with me.

Lipstick & Danger Street Team: These people are always on their game and get the word out about my work. Love you guys!

DUPED

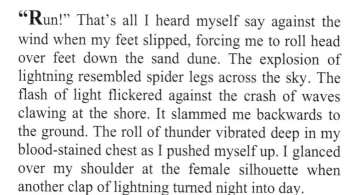

"**R**un!" That's all I heard myself say against the wind when my feet slipped, forcing me to roll head over feet down the sand dune. The explosion of lightning resembled spider legs across the sky. The flash of light flickered against the crash of waves clawing at the shore. It slammed me backwards to the ground. The roll of thunder vibrated deep in my blood-stained chest as I pushed myself up. I glanced over my shoulder at the female silhouette when another clap of lightning turned night into day.

I kicked off my remaining shoe to move faster across the wet sand while I still had a chance at escape. Rain pelted my face like icy tacks.

Don't look back, I remembered thinking, more of a motivator than anything else. The image of being carried off in handcuffs with a burly policeman, reading me my rights, flashed into my head.

Why had I gone there after the casual meeting in the village liquor store?

Simple. She was crying. What man doesn't cave at the sound of a pretty woman asking for a sympathetic shoulder after a messy divorce? That was my first mistake.

When she opened the door to her cottage, my eyes fell on a half-opened robe that revealed nothing but her birthday suit. She offered a tear-stained smile of relief. I thought an evening consoling a newly divorced female sounded like I hit the lotto. That was my second mistake.

Candlelight flickered throughout the cottage. The smell of vanilla and cinnamon nearly choked me, but I reasoned it was a small price to pay as she poured me the first of several glasses of wine. With an almost sensual abandonment, Isabel tied her robe so loose, I understood it would only be a matter of minutes before it gaped open to tease my already confused desires.

"What seems to be the problem?" Keep in mind I asked to be polite. My main focus was on that rebellious robe.

At this stage of the game Isabel had given me other things to be concerned about like, when did I brush my teeth last, should I have shaved, has my deodorant failed and why didn't I bring protection?

"I just can't believe it's over. We were married for two years. I thought he loved me." Isabel took a sip of her wine as she gazed over the rim of her glass at me. "I feel so alone. He's coming over here tonight to get a few things. I just couldn't imagine I might have to see him alone."

The third mistake slapped me upside the head, but by that time I was working on my third glass of wine. Even so, I had the good sense to realize I should leave that very instant. "I'm not sure I should be here, Isabel. He won't approve of you having a man here with the ink not dry on the divorce decree."

"He packed up boxes days ago. They're in the garage. He'll never know you're here."

She rose like a graceful swan, rising from a tranquil lake as I moved toward the door. Wouldn't you know it, that silky robe popped open, blurring the reason I thought I needed to leave. A breeze from an open window swirled the vanilla scent at me, and I was a lost cause. Those tears became magnetic as I soon found her mouth, neck and exposed shoulder. It had been a while for me and I felt more than a little unsure of myself. Isabel led me to the bedroom filled with so much candlelight I thought I'd fallen into an Indiana Jones movie.

Another glass of wine, a toast to lost love, and the sound of rain pounding on the tin roof set the scene for romance—or murder as I soon discovered.

I managed to free one foot of a shoe before Isabel ripped open my shirt like a hungry wolverine. Things were happening faster than my usual let's wait and see how the evening goes strategy. There was a fleeting thought of the World Wrestling Federation as legs and arms became entangled in impossible positions with a great deal of noises or phrases like "Oh, Gawd!"

So, when a masculine voice at the door said, "What the hell, Isabel?" I fell off the other side of the bed like a clown spilling out of a Volkswagen at the Barnum and Bailey Circus. It was in that moment I noticed the gun on the nightstand.

Isabel resembled a frightened child as she ran to

him. "I thought you'd never come. This man broke in on me. I was terrified."

"Whoa there, Isabel." I held up my hand. Somehow, I thought it might be a kind of defense shield, protecting me from the angry looking beast holding Isabel. "You invited me here because of the divorce."

"What divorce?" Those words coming from an incensed husband is never a good conversation starter, especially if he has about eighty pounds on you. With a kind of gentleness you'd save for a child, the man pushed Isabel aside and took a step toward me. "I'm going to break you in half!" he roared, forcing me to fall against the nightstand.

My fingers touched the pistol. I jerked it around and pointed. "Stop right there. This has been a terrible mistake."

When my eyes shifted to Isabel, I noticed she'd crossed her arms across her exposed chest. A playful smirk, mixed with an abundance of candlelight, managed to make the rosiness of her face appear rapturous.

"Do it, Ralph. Just like the last time. Do it. Be my hero."

I immediately understood the hulking guy was probably being manipulated. Apparently, it wasn't the first time.

"I'm going to teach you a lesson you'll never forget." That sounded like one of those phrases you hear echo over and over in a nightmare.

He lunged at me. The gun exploded a bullet into Ralph's chest. I'll never forget the feeling of blood speckling my face or the way his blood pooled against me as he fell into my arms. I know it's not manly to say I screamed, but it came out in an undignified burst as I dropped the gun on the bed.

Ralph continued his downward motion to the floor as I looked over at Isabel. Unfolding her arms, she strolled to the bed and lifted the gun.

Her smile teased me for only a second as she pointed the barrel at me. "Murderer."

Even as I watched her finger caress the trigger, I staggered out the bedroom then through the living room toward the open door. A shot rang out over my head then another that whizzed past my ear, causing me to pick up speed.

The storm knocked out cell phone reception, and who has a landline anymore? I waited all night to call the police. I should have gotten in my car and got the hell out there, but that would make me look guilty. Of course, I was guilty! I kept telling myself it was self-defense and the police would see it my way. I pictured an outcry of injustice as they led me away in an orange jumpsuit and shackles.

The next morning, I took my coffee on the deck, rehearsing my call to the police. I stood there lost in my own misery as I watched a couple stroll along the beach, toward my place. Isabel and her not-so-dead husband walked on the morning sand, arm in arm. They smiled my way and waved.

As I stood there stunned, Isabel looked back over her shoulder with a coy smile then mouthed the words, "Call me."

DEATH BY SURVEY

Nothing good ever happened to me, unless you count the time I won a free bagel every day for a month at a local coffee shop. Since I spent a ridiculous amount of money on skinny lattes there, that in fact, caused me to gain five pounds, it felt like poetic justice. Because I filled out a few questions online to get a rewards card, which led to this windfall, my confidence level in good karma convinced me I could take the survey which popped up on my Facebook account.

Before long, sets of multiple-choice questions popped up each day for me to fill out to indicate which movie star I most resembled or some other mysterious revelation to entertain me. So, I took the surveys. After all, many of my friends took the same ones. It was a harmless way to pass the time when surfing the net. Except it turned out to be a little more sinister than that.

When my friend Carla ended up in the hospital from a serious car accident, I rushed to her side. She wasn't the sharpest crayon in the box when it came to texting and driving. More than once I needed a change of underwear after being her passenger. Other than this slip in judgement, she was a straight arrow; never drank anything stronger than decaf tea, no red meat, PBS was her programming of choice and her radio was preprogrammed to NPR. Whatever the reason, she didn't make it.

"Are you family?" the police officer asked as he took out his little notepad. He patted his pocket for a pen. I handed him one from my purse.

"No. Just a friend."

"Your friend was dressed like Princess Leia— you know, like Star Wars. The hit and run driver never slowed down."

"Wait. She wore a costume?" That didn't sound like Carla. Money was tight being a librarian.

"Yes. Star Wars. Witnesses say it was a food truck. Shouldn't take long to locate it. There were a couple of things in her car you'll want to collect for the family." He skimmed through some notes then continued. "A box with a picture of Betty Davis, a gift certificate to the farmer's market on South Elm, two stuffed animals—"

"Stuffed animals?"

"A sock monkey and a panda. Why?"

"She loved monkeys and pandas. But I didn't know she had that either." I swiped at a tear trying to escape down my cheek.

He waited for a few seconds before continuing. I guess he wanted to give me a chance to compose myself. "Other things in the box were a picture of Pope Francis, a rabbit's foot and a pair of ruby slippers like that chick from the Wizard of Oz."

"That doesn't make any sense."

"I'm sorry for your loss. I'll make sure you get the box of personal items."

After having a good cry on the way to Carla's tiny apartment, I carried the box up three flights of stairs. We had exchanged keys to each other's place so getting inside wasn't that big of a deal. I set the box on her kitchen counter before turning to glance around her home.

I moved to her loveseat which she called her gigantic sofa and collapsed in the middle as another round of tears streamed down my face. Her laptop rested in an open position on the coffee table. I reached to touch the keys and it sprang to life. She didn't use a password so I quickly accessed her social media. I hoped there would be clues to where she was going dressed like a Star Wars character.

I found nothing unusual. When I clicked on Facebook a survey immediately popped up.

"What famous person in history are you?" Carla loved the surveys as much as me, and we often talked and laughed about them. In her honor I took the survey. Usually, you get an immediate answer. This time it took forever until a message appeared on the screen.

I don't think you're Carla.

"Stupid computer," I said out loud. Before I could hit the shutdown button another message appeared.

"I know who you are. Maybe you should just leave."

Needless to say, I didn't dilly-dally getting out of her apartment. Plenty of people still strolled on the street, enjoying the fall evening, so I didn't feel threatened. I mean, it was just a computer. Right?

However, on my way home I started to think about all those surveys I took.

"Guess what? Apparently, I'm a double for Ingrid Bergman." I remembered telling Carla. Thrilled to think I could be so classy; I told a number of my coworkers too.

"Ha. Well, I've got one better, darling," Carla boasted, pretending to hold a cigarette between her fingers, "I'm Betty Davis."

"And I'm most like Ariel in The Little Mermaid. Probably because I like to sing."

"I'm too nerdy for Disney. The survey I took said my personality was spot on for Princess Leia." I remembered she picked up a broom and swung it around like a light saber and knocked the lamp off my end table.

How many of those surveys had I taken over the last year? There were some on food choices, favorite animals, television shows, pets, travel destinations and even religious figures. I took all of them. I realized now it was just a way to collect information about me. Who created those surveys and why? The government? The CIA?

I hurried to my duplex and found a box from UPS sitting on the step. I shoved the door open and pushed the box in with my foot, then flipped on the light. My eyes landed on the computer sitting on the desk. I couldn't resist opening it to my usual social media hotspot.

A survey I recognized popped up. What famous person in history are you? Before I could respond to the questions, the answer appeared. "You are Cleopatra."

A lump formed in my throat as I retrieved the box and sliced through the tape. Inside the box was a picture of Ingrid Bergman, a Steak n' Shake gift card, a postcard from London showing my favorite castle, a teddy bear, and a Little Mermaid costume. There was even a picture of Cleopatra. I glanced toward my computer as it started to speak.

"Are you there? Put the mermaid costume on for me please."

I froze momentarily before taking the computer to my breakfast bar. The screen, now black, indicated it had gone to sleep. Then the monotone voice spoke a little more forcefully.

"I said, put the mermaid costume on for me please."

I stepped back and shouted. "No." I swallowed so loud it sounded like a gulp under a microphone. "No," I repeated.

The computer screen came to life once more with a soft blue light. Two men dressed in metallic suits folded their hands in front of their very thin bodies. Their elongated heads and arms reminded me of standing in front of a fun-house mirror.

"She is a little more difficult," one man commented. "This could be the one we need."

A buzzing sound emitting from the computer paralyzed my body even as I tried to shake my head in rebellion.

"Put on the mermaid costume. Do not resist."

But I continued to refuse with my mind until the computer went black, and I felt the control of my body return to me. I sucked in deep breaths while I tried to shut the computer down. Grabbing my purse, I knew I needed to escape. When I threw open the door, the two men from the computer stood in the hall staring at me.

I tried my best to shut the door, but it now felt like it weighed a thousand pounds.

"Come with us. You will return to our planet for further study. Your friend Carla took the surveys and always obeyed. She died like all the others. Now, would you like for us to call you Ingrid Bergman for your journey?"

My word of advice; don't take those social media surveys. You are being watched and not by the government, at least not our government. I won't be back.

LOVE A PIRATE

Nothing shakes a person to the core like seeing a pirate in full regalia walk into the workplace and yell, "Arrr! Ahoy, me hearties! I'm lookin' for a lass to go with me to see the world."

That's when you pull out your cutlass, or sword, and wave it about until everyone starts to rise from their cubicle and stare in disbelief. I usually point at a few confused and non-threatening men who have managed to drip some coffee on their casual Friday polo shirts. For special effect, I stomp toward them in my fancy black boots and take turns pressing my weapon against their chest, just hard enough to alert them this isn't a movie prop.

"Do either of you scallywags know of a lass named Misty Dawn?" I do a lot of growling at this point as my one good eye sneaks a glance around the gathering crowd. One dares to smirk and say there is no such person by that name.

You're probably wondering at this point how a person with a Ph.D. in Geophysics become a pirate. Funny story actually. As you can imagine, when you try speed dating at a popular restaurant, and say your job is to document, evaluate, and take measurements of geographic features and anomalies, the young lady sitting across from you, often struggles to keep from yawning. Even the ladies called cougars, can't wait for that bell to ring and move on.

One night an accident changed my life trajectory. After coming home from another miserable date to my modest house on the edge of town, I stumbled over the stray cat who always waited for a handout. Usually, I tried to coax it to come closer, but even she would saunter off like I was invisible. That night I was more interested in why my front door was ajar and the doorframe had been splintered so badly. I had a faint notion some pretty big termites had taken up residence.

I flipped on the light to find my things in disarray and someone trying to lift my new sixty-inch television off its stand. The burglar was so startled he dropped the TV and ran into the kitchen, also in disarray. The sound of my TV screen shattering, combined with eight rejections at the speed-dating event, pushed me over the edge. I guess if truth be told, having a story that I chased a burglar through my house, would be more interesting than geographic features and anomalies, if I ever met someone halfway interested in me.

Without warning, the burglar grabbed a knife out of the stainless-steel knife set I ordered off the Home Shopping Channel. (Don't judge me. Back then I didn't get out much.) The burglar grinned and jabbed at me, but I had the where withal to grab a metal tray I neglected to put away the night before, and blocked his attempt at murder. Before he could swing at me again, I smacked the tray across his face, breaking his nose. Relief washed over me as the knife fell into the sink. The old adrenaline machine was really pumping when I smacked him three more times, knocking him to the floor, where he hit his head. I heard sirens in the distance. God love nosey neighbors.

Those pretty boys in blue swarmed in and took over before said burglar rallied to put me in a headlock and traction. I forgot about the knife until the next morning when I tried to put things in order. Unfortunately, the knife had fallen down into the garbage disposal and when I turned it on, the knife became a heat seeking missile. That's how I lost my eye and found a new life.

There I was, laying in a hospital bed recovering from surgery and feeling sorry for myself when an attractive nurse stopped in and smiled. She brought me a present from her kids. Said it was left over from Halloween and after they heard about how I lost my eye, they wanted to do something for me. After she left, I opened the box. It was some tattoo sleeves of skulls, roses and crosses. I slipped them on and then I slipped on the black eye patch. Before I could sneak a peek in the mirror the night nurse came on duty. She took one look at me and arched an eyebrow.

"Well, hello."

I wanted to ask if she was getting a cold since her voice sounded kind of low and husky; much different than the last time I saw her. Needless to say, by the time I left the hospital, a whole new world had opened up for me. I quit my job, got the real tattoos, let my hair grow out because my stylist said the curls of gray were a nice touch. I started a business called, "Love a Pirate". I suddenly realized that old saying was true, "Fate doesn't ask you what you want. Fate knows what's best, even if you don't." Which brings me back to finding Misty Dawn in the workplace.

"Blimey!" I usually shouted this out in frustration. "Lass, where ya be?"

At least five women raised their hand and took a come-hither posture. This was not unusual. Since I had a picture of who I would christen Misty Dawn, I slowly examined each of the five head to toe, long enough to make them giggle and shiver with delight.

Then I saw her. Standing in the back of the office, red-haired and wearing a large pair of glasses. I stalked her in slow motion, saying I should make her walk the plank for hiding from me. By the time I reached her and pulled her into my arms, she couldn't resist a shy smile.

One more forgotten and ignored person could remember this day, that they were chosen.

DIED TOO SOON

"I told you to leave me alone," I complained, just like every night, when I tried to go to bed. It didn't make any difference. The clouded lady with outdated hair and a long dress from the 1800s still appeared in the mirror as I brushed my teeth. She would smile and shake her head no until I returned to the upstairs hall in my recently purchased house.

At first the thought of having a permanent resident, of the apparition kind, made me tingle with joy. I only saw her on stormy nights, then in my bathroom mirror, and now she had taken to reorganizing my pantry. Sometimes when I tried to find the parsley or garlic to prepare a nice dinner for my friends, I'd hear her laughing at my confusion as to what I should do. Finally, I started talking to her and she, surprisingly, talked back.

It wasn't an old lady voice, as I anticipated, but that of a young woman, full of life and mischief. Sometimes her laugh woke me from a deep sleep and I would see her standing at the foot of my bed. In the beginning, it occurred to me I might be losing my mind, until I found the note she'd written.

"I died too soon, because of deceit."

Later I asked her, what deceit? She only smiled and disappeared for a good two weeks.

I soon realized I missed her. The laugh, the smiles, the mischief, kept me entertained most evenings when I returned from work. Even when she moved my tools as I attempted a new restoration project, eventually, made me smile. But then she was gone. I regretted fussing at her and reread her note over and over. Maybe if I discovered the deceit, all would be revealed.

There was nothing to be done except research, which I did unsuccessfully until the night I found a hat box in the attic. Full of letters, valentines and ribbons, I wondered if they'd been for my ghostly lady. I fingered each item and tried to reach her spirit. It was the last velveteen box I opened with a small locket that took my breath away. Inside was a picture of my lady, no more than twenty, posed with flowers in her pretty light-colored hair. My heart ached. What had happened to one so young that she was forced to haunt this house.

An Amazon package arrived at work the next day and was left on my desk while I went to lunch. I didn't remember ordering anything, so I waited until I reached home to open it. Inside was a picture of my lady holding the hand of an older man standing next to her. On the back was written, "She died too soon." Also on the back were the names, Pearl and Ezekiel Jonas, 1889.

A Google search turned into three hours of going down various rabbit holes. Then an obscure newspaper article from 1889 revealed the answers I hadn't expected.

Mrs. Pearl Waters was found unresponsive in her home after her husband returned from a business trip in nearby Shelbyville. Further investigation was not required since it was suspected her death was a suicide. She was loved by all.

I fast-forwarded through several weeks of the newspapers, hoping to find more information. Finally, I realized something was amiss when I found the following announcement. It was a mere two weeks past her death.

Ezekiel Waters once again finds love with Miss Joanna Carl from Shelbyville. The community is invited to the wedding this Saturday at the Mount Sinai Methodist Church at noon. Refreshments to follow.

"You killed her for someone else!" I shouted. "How could you?"

I banged my fist on the table and felt my heart had broken. She was beautiful and full of life. I retrieved the locket and opened it as I'd done in her absence. Rubbing my thumb across the surface, I closed my eyes, pretending I could feel the softness of her hair.

"My dearest Pearl. I would have loved you forever. Instead, I can only love you now. Please return to me."

A gust of wind blew open my front door, as my phone sent an impending tornado alert through the airways. I hurried to slam the door shut and could already feel the spray of rain starting to pound the house.

My heart was heavy, so I turned on the television to distract myself from the realization I might never see the woman I loved again. I fell asleep, not really concerned if I'd be blown away. It wasn't until morning, when I heard a vehicle pull into my drive, that made me realize I'd slept through the storm. I pushed back the curtain on the front door and spotted an Amazon truck.

Was it something I ordered to continue the restoration? This time the driver carried nothing as I watched the person look around and back toward the steps. I walked out onto the front porch, wondering if I was going to have to assist with whatever the delivery might be.

"Morning," I yawned. "Some storm, huh?"

The driver turned around and removed her hat. Long amber colored hair fell down around her shoulders as a smile lit up her face.

Shocked, all I could say was, "Pearl."

Then she was running up the steps into my arms. I lifted her off her feet and kissed her with passion I didn't know I owned. "You're back. In person," I laughed. "I have missed you."

"Because of you, I have returned just in time."

"And not too soon for me. I love you."

"I knew you were the one to free me."

MYSTIC VOODOO PARAPHILIA AND PALM READING

Cherabella opened the door to her grandmother's Mystic Voodoo Paraphilia and Palm Reading store for the police. The back-alley business was no more than ten feet wide but boasted a depth of twenty-five feet. The neighbors in the upstairs apartment across from Mama Juju, which is what everyone called her, heard arguing the night before, a scream and maybe a gunshot. They admitted it could have been those crazy college boys shooting off firecrackers after a night of celebrating the fourth.

"Why the concern? Mama Juju argues with every customer sooner or later because she jacks up the prices on her black magic medicine and scares the crap out of them with voodoo." Officer Devaux tried to look unconcerned as the granddaughter rattled the door to make the key turn. She knew the officer visited to purchase his chicory each week. Mama Juju hinted once she added a little something to bring him back for Cherabella.

She shifted her chocolate brown eyes to him. "Mama Juju didn't call me this morning. I left a little early to swing by. By that time," she nodded at the neighbors standing on a balcony that had seen better days. "Let's just go in."

The door swung open but caught on a rug which forced the bell over the door to tinkle, almost in merriment. Little light made its way inside the large window due to the towering building across from the shop. A hint of mildew and jasmine, mixed with the smoke of extinguished beeswax candles clung to the stale air.

Cherabella loved everything about the shop; the shrunken heads hung on the walls (which were really plastic), the jars of deformed creatures soaking in formaldehyde, the bottles of magic potions that promised to trap a lover or punish an adulterer and the drawing of a palm mounted on the back wall.

"Mama Juju!" Cherabella tried to sound natural, but she couldn't help but notice Officer Devaux unsnap his holster and rest his hand on the handle of his weapon. She decided by the curious examination of his eyes drifting from oddity, to the lifting of brown bottles to sniff, he feared the voodoo more than the possibility of a crime.

"Is all this stuff real?"

"No. Mama Juju makes most of it from various teas, herbs and spices." Cherabella called again. "Hello?" Walking to the back of the store, she pulled back the lace curtain to peer into a small room her grandmother called home. "Odd."

The officer quipped. "How would you know?"

he mumbled as he clicked on his flashlight.

Cherabella ignored the insult as a moan lifted from the darkness. "Mama Juju!" Officer Devaux directed his flashlight at the floor. A boney woman pinched with wrinkles across her face, lay in a bloody pool. He pulled the chain on the light bulb that swung from the middle of the ceiling then called for an ambulance on his radio.

"Mama Juju, who did this to you?" Cherabella choked on her tears as she removed the red bandana from her grandmother's frizzy gray hair.

A hand lifted to Cherabella's face. "Read the tea leaves."

Officer Devaux kneeled down. "Mama, did a customer hurt you?"

She whispered in a strangled voice. "Tea leaves."

Paramedics arrived to rush an unconscious Mama Juju to the hospital amidst the sobs of Cherabella and police barricading curious onlookers. Officer Devaux led the granddaughter back inside as the ambulance sped away.

"Did Mama Juju read tea leaves to many clients, Cherabella?" He removed his hat to dab at the perspiration. "I'll wait here for the crime scene team if you want to get to the hospital."

"Mama Juju seldom read tea leaves. She made teas to treat ailments for older clients. Didn't believe tea leaves spoke truth but held cures." Cherabella shrugged then wiped her eyes. "Tea for colic, headaches, high blood pressure, you name it, she made it." She moved behind the counter where her grandmother kept the book of recipes. "Oh no!"

Officer Devaux joined her. "Problem?"

"Mama's recipe book for teas is missing."

"Maybe she put it somewhere else."

"No. I know it doesn't look like it, but Mama is meticulous with placement. People always wanted her recipes so she kept it all secret. Even I don't know the exact combinations."

"Why would someone shoot an old woman for a recipe book? That's just crazy." He spotted a large bowl on a dusty shelf covered with a piece of burlap. "Would she keep tea leaves in a bowl?" He reached for the burlap and jerked his hand back when a mouse scurried from behind the chipped bowl.

The front doorbell tinkled again as a well-dressed man entered.

"I'm sorry. We're closed." Cherabella tried to sound polite but couldn't resist frowning at Officer Devaux. She motioned for him to move away. "Mama Juju won't be in for a few days."

The officer ignored her and lifted the cloth to peer inside the bowl.

"Oh. I'm Carl Higgins. I paid for some medicine. Some tea, I think. I paid in advance."

What nonsense did Mama Juju use on this man? Her eyes caught a glimpse of the officer lifting a piece of paper from the bowl, then shaking tea grounds from the surface. "I'm sorry. I don't know anything about any tea."

The officer dropped the paper then drew his gun on the customer. "I think our friend here came for more than tea. Get those hands in the air."

"Good Lord, Officer Devaux, what is wrong with you?"

"There was a note in those nasty tea grounds. Looks like Mama Juju discovered a cure for Alzheimer's with one of her teas. Recipe is on that piece of paper with a warning. 'No give Higgins.'"

Cherabella's hand flew to her throat. "You're the man from the pharmaceutical company that took samples of Mama Juju's teas to test at your lab. What's the matter? Not in the recipe book you took last night?"

"I work for powerful people." His voice, although nervous, grew slow and calculated.

Cherabella rushed up to him and yanked out three hairs from his well-groomed head. She did her best to offer a diabolical smirk.

"What do you plan to do with that, young lady? My people will crush you."

"I know voodoo, Mr. Higgins. You are the one who should be worried. Confess and you'll live."

"Nonsense."

Cherabella dropped the hairs in a clear jar with some bat wings and snake venom. She spoke Cajun while waving her hands over the top, then fanned the invisible magic toward Mr. Higgins.

In seconds, he began to sweat and pull at his collar.

Officer Devaux put a hand on the man's shoulder. "You don't look so good."

"What have you done to me?" he choked.

"Confess."

He collapsed into the officer's arms. "Yes. Yes. I did it. Now make it stop," he cried.

Cherabella whispered some words over him then lifted her hands to the ceiling. Mr. Higgins soon began to breathe easier. Another ambulance arrived within a few minutes to take Mr. Higgins to the hospital.

"I didn't know you practiced voodoo, Cherabella." Officer Devaux chuckled.

"I don't. I made it up. Guess he believed it though." She winked at the officer. "Better get to the hospital. Maybe I'll have Mama Juju add a little something extra to your chicory next time you visit."

Officer Devaux opened the door for her then looked back over his shoulder. "I'll be sure to remind her. I'll give you a ride to the hospital. Maybe I'll stick around. You know, to make sure you ladies don't get into any more trouble."

"For someone who doesn't believe in voodoo, you are a cautious man."

"Yes, I am." He grinned. "You've been working a little magic on me for some time, I think."

"Nice of you to notice," she cooed. "Maybe we should talk to Mama Juju about that."

THE FAMILY BUSINESS

I was sick of it. The lying. The sneaking around. And now stealing things that were almost repulsive to me. I'd stooped to an all-time low. There was no romantic suspense any longer in drinking peach martinis and wearing skin-tight leopard pants that even a leopard couldn't squeeze into. The black leather boots and diamond earrings had lost their appeal. No one cared. Now more important things held value—like toilet paper. I remember the first time I admitted to the police what I'd done.

"You did what?" a mealy-mouthed officer chuckled. "You're a cat burglar for crying out loud. As a matter of fact, you come from a long line of cat burglars. I know because I sent your grandpa to prison. You better start from the beginning." Then along with the other uniformed men standing like mannequins in various outlandish postures, they burst out laughing making jokes about how I had soiled the family business. I found their humor a bit inappropriate.

So, I told them how the market for high end

jewelry, paintings and other non-essential do-dads had dried up for me. Gone were the days of hobnobbing with the rich and famous in order to worm my way into their hearts, deep pockets and finally their security systems. There were times I think those rich yahoos liked to brag that they'd been taken to the cleaners by a woman with the looks of an angel, the cunning of a demon and the agility of an acrobat from Cirque du Soleil. I admit, the prize was not as important as the rush of a successful escape and never leaving a clue as to my identity, although everyone suspected it was me. It was all part of the game.

The casinos closed down because of a worldwide emergency; Monaco, Las Vegas, even the Indian reservations, were on lockdown. Those high rollers were either sick, quarantined or watching the stock market plummet while they wandered aimlessly through their fancy digs. What was I supposed to do? I had to make a living. My expenses weren't going away just because of a virus. Since I worked off the books and the IRS had no idea who I was, I certainly couldn't count on any government bailout money. When life gives you lemons, you make lemonade.

It might surprise you to know there is a whole black market for paper products; napkins, paper towels, disposable plates and bowls, and even paper favors like streamers. However, toilet paper became the jewel in my crown. I switched from skin-tight leggings and boots from Paris to baggy sweatpants and tennis shoes from Walmart. That's right. I became a walking slug nobody noticed. I stopped wearing makeup, dying my hair and eating Tofu. Now there were Cheeto crumbs on my sweatshirt, and I smelled like an ashtray.

There was very little interaction with store personal, and the shoppers had this thing about social distancing that allowed me to easily slip products inside my pants, raincoat or shirt. I dismantled the security system from a computer I kept in my 2001 Buick with the two-tone paint job. It wasn't like I could drive my new Corvette and not get noticed. Slipping back inside after dark, when everyone was restocking, was child's play.

"Wait. Wait," the officer held up a hand as he bent over in laughter. "You're killing me." Once he caught his breath, he wiped a tear from the corner of his eye and insisted I continue.

Then came the night it all hit the fan. I had grabbed a chili burrito and some jalapeno poppers at the drive through along with some ice water. By the time I struggled to squeeze through the back window of the store, I realized my culinary choices of late may have affected not only my waistline, but my digestive system as well. I hurriedly stuffed the trash bags with the yet-to-be-stocked toilet paper bundles when nature hit. There was nothing to do but find a lady's room. Unfortunately, when I slipped back to the storeroom to retrieve my loot, a security guard was waiting for me.

"And then he called you guys," I admitted, as I pulled back my shoulders and tried to act unaffected by this latest plot twist.

After the laughter died down the officer in charge slapped me on the back. "Gonna let you off with a warning this time. I'm sure your old grandpa would be so proud of how you've turned out. We got bigger fish to fry than a cat burglar turned toilet paper thief." He grinned mischievously. "We're wiping your slate clean." With that everyone laughed again.

Yes. I walked out a free bird. When I got in my car, I took out the three rolls of toilet paper I found in the restroom of headquarters and smiled. I knew I'd make more off those rolls than they would make in three days. Sometimes life just stinks.

DEAD MAN'S BELLS

Law enforcement stood around the body like a Baptist minister had called a spontaneous prayer meeting. The chirping of birds and a light summer breeze, whistled through the oak tree branches against a nearby potting shed. It gave the day an ordinary feel. With a deep sigh, the sheriff nodded for the coroner to do his thing.

"What we got, Deputy Shelly?" Even after leaving Texas twenty years earlier, the sheriff still possessed a Southern drawl you could cut with a knife. A cowboy hat rested on the back of his head, something that looked out of place in this small Illinois town.

Shelly took two steps for every one of the sheriff's. "That's her, Sheriff. Mrs. Chipper, the former Mrs. Halbert and before that, Mrs. Jones." She recited the litany of facts with the emotion of reading a telephone book.

The sheriff stopped. "Three husbands?" He spotted Mrs. Chipper sitting on a garden bench amidst blooming flowers and stroking her calico cat. The blooms, so breathtakingly beautiful, caused him to chew on his words a few seconds before speaking to the deputy. "Where are the first two husbands?"

"The first husband, Mr. Jones, left town before you came here. Had an eye for the ladies. Everyone thought he ran off with another woman."

"And Mr. Halbert? Number two?" The sheriff spotted a pathetic looking man swaying back and forth near the woman; his head bowed. Mrs. Chipper paid the swaying man no mind as she stared at the calico who had had enough and jumped down into a clump of catnip.

She shrugged. "Heard they divorced."

"Did you know him?"

"No. We're ten miles from town, Sheriff. They stayed to themselves. Only came to town for supplies. Guess he moved on."

The sheriff nodded toward the body. "And Mr. Chipper? What of him?"

"Worked at the Chevrolet dealer. Sold a truck to the then Mrs. Halbert and the next thing we heard, he up and marries the woman." Shelly waved off a bee then sneezed. "I'm allergic to all these flowers."

The sheriff stopped in front of the widow. "Mrs. Chipper, I'm sorry for your loss." She lifted her eyes, but remained silent. "Shelly tells me you were away the last few days."

"Buying more plants and seeds for a new garden." She lifted her hand like a butterfly toward the many beds of profuse color. "I returned to find the police."

"A couple of boys, looking for their hunting dog,

found your husband."

"Yes." A hint of exasperation touched her voice.

The sheriff cut his eyes to the swaying man standing behind her. "He work for you?"

The woman looked over her shoulder then back to the sheriff. "He's my son. Not quite right. Hard worker. He dug all these beds for me." Her gaze drifted around the acre yard. "Each bed is a memory."

"Yes, ma'am." The sheriff excused himself to speak to the coroner. "Whatcha got for me?"

The coroner removed his gloves then wiped his forehead against his shirt sleeve. "No trauma. Probably a heart attack. He wasn't a young man. Maybe he was digging."

The sheriff looked at the mounded dirt. "Making another flower bed, I'm guessing."

He stole another look at the woman and her son. She appeared to be enjoying the early summer sun. The yellow and pink flowers behind her stood on tall stalks. His grandmother had called them "Dead Man's Bells" or foxglove flowers. He was warned not to be tempted to stick his finger in the little blossoms that looked like finger caps. Of course, he had tried it anyway and was rewarded by a bee sting under his fingernail. Later his grandmother warned of other dangers.

"Heart attack, huh?" The sheriff pooched out his bottom lip then strode over to Mrs. Chipper. "These are beautiful flowers, Mrs. Chipper." He pointed to the ones behind her. "Are those foxgloves?"

Her face brightened. "Yes. They are handy to have around."

"Especially if you want to kill someone." The sheriff watched Mrs. Chipper stand and dust off her faded jeans before carefully adjusting her wide-brimmed hat.

"How did you know?"

"Digitalis is a toxin that comes from foxglove. Overdoses can induce a heart attack. How did you give it to him?"

"I left him tea." She took a deep breath. "Would you like for me to tell you about the other flower beds now?" Again, the smile. "He isn't the only one, you know."

"Yes, Mrs. Chipper. I would appreciate your help." The sheriff held his arm out for her.

She eased up next to him to slip her hand into place. "Well, aren't you a dear? Perhaps later we can have some tea."

WHO KILLED DAD

It remained a mystery to everyone but me. I knew the killer, but no one would listen to a teenager who stuttered and had a propensity to exaggerate to get a point across. Finally, I just stopped talking. After all he wasn't my dad. As far as I knew he wasn't anyone's dad. That was just what everyone called him; Dad. I'm not sure why. Later I understood the name came from taking in so many foster children. The neighbors thought he must be a good man.

I knew better. Behind closed doors he trained us to be pick-pockets, panhandlers and shoplifters. I'd be the front guy and ask a clerk or shopper about some item, all the while, stuttering my head off. I felt sorry for the mark because they really were trying to be patient with me and listen.

Then that kid arrived with the clean-cut look of someone with money and brains. Only he was just like us, except he'd come from China and he actually had two parents in jail instead of one. His name was Hunan which turned out to mean cuisine. Quiet and obedient, the new kid didn't fit in at first, but I later realized he was evaluating how to take over the group. Because of his Asian accent some of the others made fun of him. I understood not being able to speak all that well, so I befriended him. We became inseparable.

Like all of us kids living with Dad, Hunan had a quirky, dark side. He'd laugh at all the wrong places in a horror movie when the rest of us would cry, cover our faces or leave the room. He told the little ones that green olives were really eyeballs that Dad took from the children who didn't obey. Little Sarah became so frightened to eat the food Dad provided for us that I had to break ranks with Hunan.

"Stop scaring our little sister," I demanded. Of course, it took me a good five minutes to get it out because I was a little intimidated by his quiet, somber glare at me. He started to mock my speech impediment. Thankfully, Dad walked in and got an ear full from the other kids.

"Listen, Hunan. You have to get along, or I'll send you away. You have it good here. I'm teaching you a skill." Dad felt proud of how he'd raised us to be thieves.

"Skill?" Hunan snickered. "You're a loser just like all these kids. You should put me in charge. I could raise this bunch of brats better than you. They are a disgrace."

"That is enough. No supper for you tonight. I'm calling the social worker in the morning. We don't need you."

For a second, I saw a flash of remorse in Hunan's eyes. I almost felt sorry for him. "Give him another chance, Dad." I think my stutter helped

Hunan because Dad patted me on the head and agreed.

Sullen and strangely quiet, Hunan became very obedient in the following days. I grew concerned when I noticed how he watched Dad's every move, as if plotting mischief. The look of contempt in his narrow eyes frightened me enough that I tried to keep a closer watch on the little ones in our group. Hunan began to whisper to them about taking their eyeballs when Dad went away if they didn't do what he wanted.

"Dad needs to go," he told me one night. "It's him or me."

"Not possible," I commented. "What would happen to us? This is my family."

"We'll see. I gotta plan."

In the morning I found Dad dead on the floor. The police came when I fetched the neighbor lady down the hall. I kept saying over and over, "Hu killed Dad!" I got a number of pats on the shoulder; a neighbor dropped some granola bars by for us to munch on and several policemen told me they didn't know who killed Dad.

"Blunt force trauma, I'm guessing," I heard the detective say as he entered the living room where us kids huddled on the couch, except for Hunan. He sat on a stool, looking out the window with a smirk on his face. "Any of you kids know who might have killed your dad?"

I nodded. "Hu-Hu killed Dad."

The detective kneeled down by me and smiled. "It's okay son, we'll find who did this. You're the oldest. Was there trouble with a neighbor or a friend?"

I pointed to Hunan. I took each word as slow as possible. "Who. Killed. Dad."

All the other kids started nodding and pointing as Hunan turned his head in our direction and started eating some olives out of a jar. The detective stood up and chewed his bottom lip before taking a step toward Hunan. "Do you know who killed Dad?"

He popped the last olive eyeball in his mouth. "I'm Hu. And you better not cross me."

UNRESOLVED ISSUES

"If you don't tell him, I will!" she screamed at the mirror. It was disgusting how simple words could have such devastating consequences. The sound of a door slamming shut indicated she was alone. The gravity of knowing too much about her father-in-law's business paled at the realization her husband had stolen, or in his words "borrowed" a half of million dollars to pay his gambling debts.

It was a crime. If he didn't pay the debt, the Russians would collect in ways she found distasteful. Would they hurt her husband? After twenty-five years of marriage maybe that wouldn't be a bad thing. He'd cheated on her with a roulette table for years. Now he was going to have to face the music. Pay the piper. Literally. The father that spoiled his only son would be heart broken.

Why hadn't he said the magic words "I'm sorry"? She looked back in the mirror and knew why. He didn't love her enough to give up the mistress that lurked in smoky rooms filled with tinkling one arm bandits and poker games that probably were rigged.

"The house always wins!" she'd warned. But he became deaf to any reason long ago.

She needed another life. Was there anything worth taking? No children to mourn her. An elderly mother with Alzheimer's would fade in and out to avoid caring. Maybe her patients would miss her, but only until they got on with their lives. Why live like this? It was all too much. Something rose up inside her after the decision of ending it all became a possibility.

The thought of all the unresolved issues in her life felt lighter with a step toward taking control. Three days. Maybe four. She would open the door to chaos. Then she would be free.

Her abandoned car was found in a creek bed under an overpass fifteen miles from the house. It was empty. When the police showed up to tell the husband, he broke down and cried for the first time in years. They told him her purse and wallet were found in the backseat, and there had been signs of a struggle. DNA tests would be run on the blood found at the scene, but it didn't look good. Did he know of anyone who had a grudge against his wife?

The husband at first promised she was a sweet, loving nurse that everyone loved. But soon the police returned and asked about his gambling debts in front of his father. Heated words ensued until the police separated the two men. It wasn't until the police accused the husband of having something to do with the missing wife that he admitted the Russians might have sent him a message.

Months passed with the dedicated wife still

missing. The police ruled out the Russians being involved fairly quickly. Now they methodically began building a case against the husband, having discovered a life insurance policy on his wife for a million dollars. It had been taken out three days before her disappearance. His life began to crumble.

Six months later a woman walked along a beach in Costa Rica. The ebb of blue water washing over her tanned feet slowed her morning routine to let a baby turtle find his way to freedom. She smiled as a breeze shifted the long floral skirt up so that her hands dropped down against it. A man waited for her on a blanket nearby. He smiled as she approached.

"You slept in." She couldn't help but smile down at his unshaven chin and bare chest.

He patted the blanket next to him and spoke after she sat down. "I rolled over and you were gone. You wore me out."

"Sorry."

"I'm not complaining." He leaned over and kissed her cheek. "I made breakfast. Should I bring it out here?"

She loved the heavy accent. "Yes," was all she needed to say?

She leaned back on her hands as the friend rose and disappeared into the small bungalow she'd rented for months. It was a good life. Carefree. The coffee shop in town she'd started for tourists was doing well. There wasn't a lot of money but there was enough. Her friend came down every month to collect on the business loan she'd secured before leaving the states. They'd become more than friends.

The time of reflection on what she did grew faint with every sunrise. She could hear Yuri singing inside. A smile appeared, knowing her husband would be surprised that she was so happy. Yuri had brought the news that he'd been arrested.

She'd gone to the Russians with her plan and they took pity on her. The money she'd squirreled away for three years was enough to rent another car, buy a plane ticket to Costa Rica and new identification papers. They had someone draw her blood to leave in the car and an expert computer technician to create the insurance policy. Yuri had rented her car so there would be no connection. He'd even been sent to pick her up at the overpass. The Russians knew, with the police involved, their money probably would never be recovered. Sending a man to prison would be a lesson for others who dared cheat them.

It wasn't until Yuri came to pick up the first payment that a friendship formed, then something else. She'd gambled on unresolved issues and won. Life was good.

ONE STEP FOREVER

One more step, I continued to tell myself. Nothing to it. You can do this. But doubts nagged me with each step forward in spite of knowing my child, Molly, needed me. She'd been taken when we journeyed through the cloud forest I discovered by chance while working on my dissertation on indigenous people of Borneo. Let me back up and explain.

Two days earlier, we became separated from my guide and pack animals when crossing a stream. I turned around and they'd vanished before my eyes. For whatever reason I called out, knowing something beyond my reason followed, and there wasn't one thing I could do about it. My gut forced me to reach for my rifle secured in its holster on the saddle. But the horse danced sideways away from me causing Molly, who remained in the saddle, to squeal with child-like delight.

"Easy girl," I consoled, even though the mare's ears laid back and her eyes searched the area behind us.

At my touch, she bobbed her head then allowed me to mount behind Molly. In seconds a breeze moved through the twisted branches of the montane forest, now shrouded in a mystic fog. I glanced behind me to ensure my eyes hadn't played tricks on me. Outlines of something followed us. Chills inched up my spine as I raced our horse away with little encouragement. Even the beast knew we were not alone. Was it the wind or voices I heard? Either way I needed to find my way back to camp. I glanced over my shoulder one more time and we had evaded whatever stalked us. Molly giggled and waved goodbye to whatever had been cloaked by the thick forest.

For weeks I'd tried to make contact with a mysterious people found in journals written by Englishman by the name of Dr. Henry in 1972. It was carried out by his guide who claimed to have escaped after he discovered a bridge shrouded in the cloud forest. He refused to lead anyone back to the doctor. He claimed the Englishman was being held captive by a race of red giants who could become one with the forest. Under continued pressure by local authorities, the man vanished and the story soon ended.

Except for the journal.

It lay for twenty years in a museum archive, until I found it. By now the stories had turned into a legend of man-eating goblins and bloodsuckers. The journal mentioned a pathway-to-nothing to reach the land of the Kanesi; a tribe of large brown people who wore red. Finding someone to lead the way took a great deal of money, promises, and a few pigs.

Rain kept me in camp for a couple of days after that first encounter. I knew trying to return to civilization would have to wait. There continued to be a presence of—something on the edge of our camp. My daughter would walk toward the thick forest at times. When I cautioned her to stay close, she would wave and smile toward things I could not see.

"Look, Momma. Aren't they pretty?"

"What? I don't see anything?"

Finally, the rain let up and I decided to pack up what I could in a small bag. With detailed directions on the location of our camp, I hoped to return the next season. We set off early and by midafternoon, I was tired and the horse needed a rest as well. This was a good place to stop. Molly loved her imaginary friends and wanted to tell me about these new ones following us. I pushed her nonsense to the back of my more reasonable self. The horse stared in the direction she'd waved, but remained calm as I reached into the saddlebags for a snack to give her and a map for me.

"Momma, I want to play."

"In a minute, baby girl. Momma has to look at the map."

I looked up from the map and she was gone. Just like that. My reason for living had been taken from me by some cruel trick of the imagination. I called out her name. Then screamed.

The horse shied from my sudden outburst then bolted through the fog settling around me like a wet blanket.

I was alone.

A red arrow appeared on the tree next to me. I followed. Every ten to twenty feet another one appeared like magic. I could see the faint outline of someone or something moving ahead of me. I could also hear the laughter of Molly in the distance.

I watched as the swinging bridge formed from rickety planks, caked in moss, bounced with someone I couldn't see. I had no idea how far the bridge stretched over a cloud-shrouded gorge, but I could hear water falling. The rope railing felt slimy in my hands as I proceeded into the mist. The slippery boards slowed me down. When I reached the other side, I collapsed only to notice the bridge in which I'd come had disappeared.

A path began to form as the mist parted enough for me to stumble forward. When I fell against a tree, I felt a hand under each arm lift me and carry me forward. In seconds, I was pulled into a clearing where dozens of stick houses formed avenues for beautiful flowers, and children played with macaque monkeys. Molly waved joyfully. "We're home, Momma."

"Hello," came a cheerful English accent. The hands released me just as the seven-foot-tall men covered in red paint came into focus and meandered toward the village. This new man extended his hand. "I'm Dr. Henry. I've been waiting a long time for you."

Molly ran to join them and hugged her around the waist. "Can you see them now?"

That day began an adventure I continue to explore with Dr. Henry and Molly, taking one step at a time—forever.

SHORT STORIES
THAT BECAME BOOKS

TURNBACK CREEK

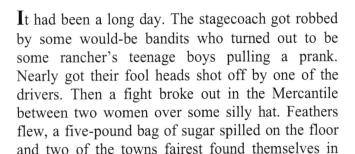

It had been a long day. The stagecoach got robbed by some would-be bandits who turned out to be some rancher's teenage boys pulling a prank. Nearly got their fool heads shot off by one of the drivers. Then a fight broke out in the Mercantile between two women over some silly hat. Feathers flew, a five-pound bag of sugar spilled on the floor and two of the towns fairest found themselves in front of the sheriff to explain their behavior.

Sheriff Conroy was a tall drink of water with a propensity to stare in the distance when you talked about a problem. He seemed to chew on the solution a few minutes before spitting out an answer. The lopsided hat would come off so he could wipe a damp brow, followed by seconds of squinting at the person with the problem. Sometimes it was intimidating enough for the person doing the complaining to decide to drop the matter. Other times the sheriff would give several options.

"Do you want me to shoot him or wound him?" The sheriff would raise his eyebrows in expectation.

"It's not that serious, sheriff."

"Let me know when it is. You have a good day, now." He would saunter off, eyes roaming the streets for trouble like he expected the James Gang to ride into town.

Until young Pastor McKenna eased into his office like a kid who had been caught with his hand in the sugar bowl, the sheriff thought he'd not have to leave town.

"Sheriff Conroy?"

"Afternoon, Pastor McKenna. Somebody been dippin' in the offering plate again?" The sheriff propped his boots on the empty desk top and pushed his hat back with one finger.

"No. No. Nothing like that. It's Miss Sinclair. She is missing." A nervous chuckle and a shrug followed.

"The born-again saloon girl? Fine figure of a woman."

"Well, she didn't return today to clean the church, and she wasn't at services yesterday."

"No crime in missing church once in a while. I do it all the time."

The pastor tried to smile, but it came across a little weak. "So, I've noticed. It's just she wasn't feeling well on Friday, and she lives out there all by her lonesome. Thought maybe someone should go check on her."

"Like me?"

"Isn't that your job?"

"My job is to keep the peace. You're the shepherd of the flock. Why don't you go?"

"It wouldn't be proper with her being single and

me being—well…"

"A man of God?" The sheriff smirked and stood up.

"I was going to say single as well. You know how people gossip."

"That I do. I heard tell the two of you were kind of sweet on each other."

"I am fond of Miss Sinclair, but I am already engaged to a lady from Kansas City. She should be here in a few days. Just graduated from a lady's preparatory school. Very educated."

"Wanted to head out to Turnback Creek to do a little night fishing anyway. I'll swing by and see how the lady is doing. She's good to visit the folks on the reservation. Maybe she headed out there."

The sheriff rode out of town at dusk on his Appaloosa. Some folks liked to tease him about his horse because, not only was it ugly, it had the temperament of a hungry mountain lion. He never worried about someone stealing him because if they tried, they'd end up at Dr. Michaels' to be patched up. There were times the animal didn't even like him, and he'd saved the cantankerous beast from quicksand. Together they bonded in friendship that had limitations on patience and who was really in control.

One thing both of them enjoyed was a ride through the countryside in the evening. No problems to solve. No chasing down some drunken cowboy with romance on his mind. No would-be rustlers who preyed on hard working people. Now the sweet, monotonous chorus of whippoorwills and crickets filled the night as he approached a one-room cabin near Turnback Creek where he hoped to catch a few bass for his late supper.

Maybe Miss Sinclair would have one of her pies she'd share with him over a cup of coffee. She sold pies to the restaurant in town and made a few cakes for local ranchers throwing big parties. It hadn't been easy after finding God and turning her life around. He'd noticed she'd put some meat on those bones the last few months. Guess someone had to sample all those sweets she made. She was still easy on the eyes and turned more than one head of a respectable husband.

"Miss Sinclair?" The sheriff knocked on the door then peered in the window of a dark cabin. He walked around back and noticed the door standing open. He called again.

A full moon rolled out from behind the clouds and seemed to bounce through the sky. The sheriff saw in the evening light very little had been disturbed in the yard. Some towels, and a sheet still lifted on the night breeze as if to free themselves from the clothesline. He pushed the door open with the toe of his boot then cocked his head to listen. Once more he called out the young woman's name but got no response.

He lit the lamp on the mantle then carried it around the room to search for clues of something gone wrong. Two dresses still hung in the closet. A patchwork quilt he recognized from the bazaar auction was folded neatly on a nearby chair, but the threadbare blanket appeared crumpled and in disarray in the middle of the bed. Maybe she wasn't a tidy housekeeper. Until the last year, those kinds of particulars hadn't meant much in her profession.

Something caught his eye on the sheet and he reached down to tug the blanket away. A pool of blood, now nearly dry. He dropped it and pivoted to examine the room with new interest. The stove felt cool to the touch indicating the restaurant would not be receiving fresh pies this week.

He blew out the light and returned to the front yard. The Appaloosa bobbed his head and stomped his hooves; a sign Sheriff Conroy recognized as an uneasiness in the animal. A gentle hand to his neck and a promise of a treat, settled the horse down enough for the sheriff to go to the barn.

The buckboard Ms. Sinclair drove into town each day was gone and so was the old nag she called a horse. The blacksmith gave her one of his when his wife insisted, he get rid of such an embarrassment. He checked the laundry, now snapping in the wind like a whip. The sheriff examined one of the towels and noticed a large dark stain. The other items also appeared to have suffered a severe scrubbing against a washboard. He guessed morning light would suggest more of the same. Everything looked as if she'd be coming back soon.

Nothing could be done tonight. He'd wait around for a while to see if anyone showed up; maybe downstream near the bridge. No use passing up a rare opportunity to catch his dinner. Before he left town, he fetched his bedroll and some things he'd need to cook his supper. If Miss Sinclair left for the weekend, she might return by daylight. Except for the bed, those stains could be anything. That bridge over Turnback Creek made enough noise when someone came over it, the sheriff wasn't too worried about anyone sneaking across.

The first two fish got released due to their size. He was a patient man. The big one would bite. They always did and he'd be ready. Just like whatever happened to Miss Sinclair, he'd get to the bottom of it. At least the wind died down and the moon now could expose anything unusual.

With the decision not to light a fire, the sheriff wrapped the blanket around his shoulders to protect against the dropping spring temperatures. He gave up trying to catch his dinner after a few hours then retrieved some biscuits and sausage from his saddlebags. Using a stump for a backrest, the sheriff settled in to enjoy his meal when his horse shied and took a step closer.

The rattle of a wagon alerted the sheriff he needed to take a stand. Navigating the slippery rocks along the creek, he arrived in time to witness the wagon pull up short. The horse moved one more step until the driver pulled the brake. The light of the moon reflected off white petticoats that were exposed when a woman climbed down. She paused a few seconds by leaning her head on something he couldn't see.

Curiosity got the best of him, causing him to move nearer to the bridge, so he had to look straight up. She moved to the back of the wagon and took out a travel case. He pondered why she decided to open it and look inside. A desperate cry of pain escaped her as she lifted something out then replaced it before securing it once more.

She picked up the case and carried it to the edge. The sheriff heard the words, "Forgive me."

With one gentle push, the case tumbled down into the water. The splash shocked the sheriff even as his eyes sought to see where it landed. He waded out a few feet before hearing a gunshot. Looking up, he watched the woman fall silently into the water. He felt frozen with a kind of fear he'd never known.

The current floated her to within inches of him. He grabbed her arm and pulled her to shore. He stared down into her face with shock. "Miss Sinclair," he whispered.

Something spooked the Appaloosa and he neighed so loudly, it echoed across the water. Another sound reached him, making him wonder about the possibility of ghosts or maybe even the spirit of Miss Sinclair. He cocked his ear and heard it again. The moonlight touched something floating in the water. Was it the travel case? Why would she throw it in the water? Did she think she'd need extra clothes in the afterlife?

The sheriff waded out waist deep into the water where the case had wedged between two rocks. He snatched it up and carried it above the water until he reached the shore. Sitting it down next to the very dead Miss Sinclair, he popped the fasteners and threw back the top. When the contents moved, he jumped to his feet. It took a second to realize a newborn baby lay inside.

He lifted it up to discover Miss Sinclair had given birth to a little girl with dark hair. The little rosebud mouth touched him in a way he hadn't expected. The water hadn't seeped inside the case yet, so he managed to wrap the child up long enough to make a fire and dry out his own clothes. He remembered a couple nearby who could help him.

When he checked for anything else he might need in the case, he found a note.

I loved you, but it wasn't enough.
You lied to me.
Now, you'll marry someone else.
Our child was to be a new beginning.

The sheriff folded it with care and made his way to the couple who lived on the edge of the reservation. They welcomed the sheriff and listened to the tragic story of the woman and child. A former Confederate soldier, the man had been taken in by his future wife's people. They'd fallen in love, and he never went home. He agreed to help the sheriff bury Miss Sinclair while his wife took care of the child.

When Sheriff Conroy rode back into town the next day, he felt relief when his deputy announced he'd slept all night without any incidents demanding his attention. The only news he could share of any consequence was about the New Hope Church inviting the whole town to meet Pastor McKenna's future bride at the potluck lunch. Normally the sheriff enjoyed these events. But then the deputy told him the rest of the news.

"The preacher man must be really in love, if you know what I mean," he winked. "Plans on having

Judge Henry perform the ceremony tomorrow night. Reception to follow." The deputy turned to leave then whirled around. "Oh, did you find Miss Sinclair? She was supposed to make the wedding cake."

Sheriff Conroy put his hands on his hips and stared out the window a little longer than usual before letting out the air he'd been holding in his chest. "She's gone."

"You sure?"

"Pretty sure." The sheriff announced he planned to make rounds then go congratulate the new couple on their wedding plans. "I'll let them know about the cake."

Clouds rolled in followed by a spring thunderstorm. The dusty streets quickly turned to mud inviting little boys to jump in and out of the puddles, in spite of their mothers' threats. Sheriff Conroy found Pastor McKenna at the church giving his bride-to-be a tour of the church and parsonage. Introductions were brief followed by an awkward silence until the pastor suggested the young lady take a second look at her new home.

"How can I help you, Sheriff?"

"Thought you'd like to know Miss Sinclair will not be returning. Your little problem has been taken care of, thanks to her untimely death."

Pastor McKenna collapsed onto a pew and covered his eyes. The sheriff handed him the note. He waited like a gunslinger waits to see his victim flinch before he pulls the trigger.

"Guess there won't be a cake," he stuttered.

"A cake? That's what you're worried about? You

hypocrite." The sheriff smacked the pastor upside the head with the palm of his hand. "That woman needed you this weekend and you let her down. She was a good woman."

"I turned my back on her."

"And your child."

"If I could change things, I would, Sheriff."

Sheriff Conroy replaced his hat and stormed out of the church. He left word for the deputy to take over until he returned. He needed some rest. Do a little fishing at Turnback Creek.

The truth was he wanted to put flowers on Miss Sinclair's grave. She was buried in the meadow near the reservation on his friend's property. She'd once taken them in when a sudden snowstorm hit and they couldn't reach home. The favor needed to be repaid. But the baby... The sheriff needed to decide soon.

The wedding reception moved outside, after the wedding vows, with plenty of music and desserts. The bride looked lovely and serene in her wedding dress. The pastor smiled and nodded like a strutting rooster with a yard full of hens, until he saw Sheriff Conroy ride up carrying something in his arms.

Throwing his leg over the saddle, he slid easily to the ground. His large finger peeled back the little blanket her mother wrapped her in the day she entered the world. People started to stare at him. His reputation leaned more toward gun play and playing cards. What he carried now made him step carefully.

"What you got there, Sheriff?" asked one of the feisty ladies from the Mercantile fiasco.

"A sweet little girl," he cooed, like a proud father. "Found her abandoned at Turnback Creek."

A gasp ran through the crowd with a number of ladies crowding in to get a peek. They immediately started some kind of baby talk until the sheriff had had enough and moved toward the newlyweds.

"Thought maybe you could baptize her, Pastor McKenna. It would mean a lot."

Before he could give his answer, his new wife took the child in her arms. The rapturous look of love filled the woman's eyes. "Josiah, we need to raise this child. I just know it." She raised up on her tiptoes and kissed him on his cheek. "Please?"

Sheriff Conroy nodded then tipped his hat. He locked eyes with the pastor and pointed his finger like a loaded gun. "I'll be watchin' you. Take care of my goddaughter, Pastor."

The new father gazed down at his daughter. "Thank you, Sheriff."

"Someday you come fishing with me at Turnback Creek. I got a heap of things to get off my chest. Like to show you a few things, too."

"Yes. I'd like that."

The sheriff left the reception and returned to Turnback Creek. Maybe he'd catch his supper this time.

THE LOST GOLD
OF WELLS FARGO

---◆◇◆---

Dust swirled around the Wells Fargo Coach resembling a ghostly apparition as it rolled toward Carson City. The sun disappeared behind a few moisture-laden clouds from time to time, but had no effect on the heat that continued to bake the landscape of boulders, scrub and pine trees clinging to the slopes of the hills. The driver slowed the team of horses to navigate a tricky area known for being narrow and slippery when rain fell or slick when the snows came in winter. Neither of those events had occurred in some time, leaving only the possibility of bandits, mountain lions or Mule deer that often wandered into the high desert from time to time.

In this part of the country there had always been a lot of places for unscrupulous men to hide and take advantage of travelers, especially since the

Comstock Lode made men either rich or greedy. Dangerous times prompted Wells Fargo to arm their drivers with the best; a sawed-off 12 or 10-gauge double-barreled shotgun, loaded with buckshot. This proved effective against pursuing riders. Today the drivers were extra vigilant since three important passengers rode along from the company, all armed and thought to be as dangerous as any would-be outlaw who tried to take the sixty-two thousand dollars in gold they carried to Carson City.

"Why are we stopping?" One of the passengers stepped down and stretched.

"Time to rest the horses and let them drink." The lead driver nodded toward a small cabin. "This swing station will swap horses for us. Need fresh ones for the rest of the trip. If we find ourselves needing to outrun anybody, then we'd be more likely to make it to Carson City."

The passenger dusted his vest and then his pants with his hat before squinting toward a hunched over man and a young woman leading some horses out of the corral next to the barn. He favored one leg and might have been tall in his younger days. Gray, stringy hair fell to his shoulders. His tattered hat shaded his face enough to make the sparse beard appear dirty.

"Was getting worried 'bout you boys. Thought maybe them outlaws got you somewhere along the line." He turned to the young woman and lifted his chin toward the cabin. "Git some food on the table, Rosie."

She released the two horses to one of the drivers and hurried off as instructed. The aroma of chicken and dumplings wafted out the door she left open in hopes of cooling the large room. The early morning chill now had been replaced by the need to swing open several windows. The biscuits, pushed to the back of the stove, were drizzled with butter and honey as the dying embers warmed the iron skillet. The two gooseberry pies sat on the shelf on the cupboard with the third one hidden for her and her pa.

By the time Rosie had the table set and the coffee steaming on the stove, the five men meandered inside, inhaling the goodness that awaited them.

"Thank you, ma'am. Sure smells good." Rosie knew the driver as Frank. He wasn't that much older than her, maybe ten years. Although polite and always told her how pretty she was getting, she rarely spoke to him.

"Don't you go makin' eyes at Jim's gal. He don't like it." The older driver, but not by much, appeared to be always ready to defend her honor. Her pa said it was because it was his way of making a good impression, like he'd be able to take care of her in a pinch. She only called him Mr. Pritchett and sometimes offered him a smile, especially if he brought her a book or writing paper.

The men found a place at the table but waited for Rosie's pa to say grace before they helped themselves to the pot of food on the table with the biscuits. Talk about the gold, news in Virginia City and unrest among some of the Apache further south dominated the conversation. The topic turned to the growing problem of marauders.

"Last stage through were hit by a group. Maybe five or six of them," Pa announced, while continuing to chew his biscuit, leaving a trail of honey to ooze from the corner of his mouth.

"Did you see them?" asked one of the passengers, as he absentmindedly put his hand on his revolver.

"Nah. Do see a couple of stray Indians around once in a while, lookin' for food. Always give them somethin'. Last week a Mexican came with them. Rosie cooked them some food and they ate outside. Never knew when they left."

The five men glanced at Rosie, who quickly diverted her eyes toward the stove. "Pa, should I feed the horses?"

"Yep. Rub 'em down too, if ya would. They look rough." Rosie nodded, removed her soiled apron and headed out the door as her father continued. "Rosie's a good girl. Needs a husband. I ain't getting' no younger and I want to make sure she's takin care of if somethin' happens to me." Rosie heard some laughter as she ran to the barn.

The smell of hay and manure traveled on the breeze that went from the front to the double doors in the back that had been slid wide open. Her sudden stop caused a small cloud of dust to swirl around her feet. The doors had been closed earlier. Sunlight threaded through the cracks in the walls and her horse stomped nervous hooves until she reached in the stall and spoke softly.

With the sudden movement in the hayloft, she remembered the cat with the five kittens. Maybe she was hunting. If the Wells Fargo men left any of the chicken and dumplings, she'd bring her some. Scooping up grain for each horse, one at a time, would make grooming them easier. The grain bin sat near the rear doors and next to the ladder leading to the loft. As she removed the lid and dug her scoop deep into the grain, a thud hit the ground behind her.

When she whirled around, Ricardo Sanchez stood a breath away, grinning like a mischievous schoolboy who wanted to pull her red braids that fell down across her breasts. Rosie fell back against the barrel and before she could call out, he jerked her into his naked arms and kissed her hard.

He released her with a burst of laughter. Rosie stepped back and dragged her calico sleeve across her mouth. "You scared me." She frowned.

Ricardo continued to smile, and this time he pulled her gently into his arms, kissing her with more passion than brute force. "Better?"

"Much better." She smiled, laying her palms against his chest. "Why are you dressed like an Indian?" Her hands went to the band around his forehead then stroked his long black hair that fell past his neck.

"This way your Wells Fargo men will not look for Mexican marauders." His hands slid down her shoulders then her arms, before taking liberties with her backside as he enjoyed her neck and shoulder with his mouth.

Rosie pushed him away. "Stop."

"That is not what you usually say to me. I love you, Rosie. We will marry soon."

A sigh followed as she wrapped her arms around

him. "And I love you. But there are extra men today. Three more. You need to be careful."

"Must me a big haul."

"Sixty-two thousand in gold." She kissed him then patted his cheek. "You'd better go."

"My men are waiting." With a final embrace, he backed outside, winking at her when he reached his horse. "Be ready to leave when I come for you."

~ ~ ~ ~

The Wells Fargo men loaded up and were soon on their way when Rosie finished taking care of the horses. Several compliments on the food got only a shy smile and a nod from her. To look them in the eye when she knew what awaited them, gave her a sense of guilt, but not enough to warn them. Ricardo promised he'd not hurt anyone like the other two times. This time might be different. These Wells Fargo men resembled gunslingers or soldiers; men used to hitting their target. With Ricardo's growing reputation, it made sense that powerful men would protect the wealthy investors.

Rosie's father came to stand next to her and shifted his weight from one leg to the other. "Guess they know what they're doin'. Sure a lot of gold on that stage." When she didn't respond, he continued. "It wouldn't hurt you to be a little nicer to those young fellas. You need a husband to take care of you."

"I don't need no man to take care of me," she snapped. "Besides, nobody does that now. Why, I do most of the work around here, including takin' care of you, Pa." Folding her arms across her chest, she dared cock her head and level an angry glare at him. "I'll find my own man."

"You mean like that wild Mexican who sneaks in to see you? Think I didn't know about that?" She huffed a sound of irritation and pivoted to leave, but he grabbed her arm with the grip of a much younger man and jerked her around to face him. "He fancies those blue eyes and long red hair. I'll blow his head off if he touches you."

"You're too late," she said jerking free. "We're goin' to get married and leave this place. I want to see somethin' besides mule deer and mountain lions. I want to wear pretty dresses and look like a grown-up woman instead of a ranch hand that has to wear a man's britches to shovel manure out of a horse stall."

"And you think that good for nothin' is goin' give you that? Why, he's poorer than Job's turkey, I tell ya. He's probably one of those outlaws the Wells Fargo men been talkin' about. If you'd stick around to listen, you'd know that."

Taking a deep breath, Rosie let it out slowly to calm herself. "I love him, Pa. Please."

"No. You're my only child and I'll not let you throw your life away. You want city life? Fine. I'll send you to Virginia City next coach headed that way. My sister will take you in."

Rosie kicked up some dirt with the toe of her boot in a show of rebellion but doubted he'd remember his promise. Storming toward the house to clean up after the men, she decided right then and there, someday she'd be giving the orders, not a man.

~ ~ ~ ~

Ricardo Sanchez ordered his men to several locations along the route through a section of the road that climbed a steep hill then flattened out for one hundred yards. The next few miles meandered gently downward through some of the last remaining pinon forests. They had built a dam of rocks against a hillside weeks earlier and needed only to jam a beam they'd secured beneath the pile to start the thunderous motion. Two Pulls, a Washoe Indian from the Tahoe Region, whistled the signal, the stage had been spotted.

With more grunting and muscle than Ricardo had anticipated needing, the dam cracked, releasing the avalanche of rock and timber that blocked its path. It sprawled haphazardly across the road. If the Wells Fargo Men had been on horseback, they could have easily navigated their way around the debris field. These kind of unexplained rampages of nature was usually explained by too much rain or snow and the occasional shaking of the ground.

The rattle sound of the coach and the thundering hooves of the horses melted with the driver's voice that now tried to slow them down. Ricardo glanced at the positions of his five men as Two Pulls joined him. With his dark skin and clothing, he could easily pass for a Washoe brother. Smiles were exchanged between them as the coach rolled to a stop. Now they only had to watch, listen and wait.

Men jumped out of the coach and leveled their

shotguns, anticipating trouble. When none came, they inspected the rockslide.

"Now ain't this somethin'," the driver, Mr. Pritchett groaned. "Think we can get enough of these moved to pass? Don't want to be here after dark."

"Couple hours ought to do it." Frank, the backup driver said, pushing his hat back with one finger. "We could hitch the horses to some of these and make better time. Some of the smaller ones we can roll out of the way."

"Better get at it. Shouldn't have had that second piece of Rosie's gooseberry pie. Weighing heavy on me now." One of the Wells Fargo men rubbed his belly.

"Come to think of it, my gut doesn't feel so good," another company man confessed.

Mr. Pritchett removed his vest. "Sounds to me like you're a couple of little girls not wantin' to help. Maybe if you weren't wearin' those layers of fancy clothes, you'd have more room for that pie to spread itself around a bit. You fellas better decide right now if you're goin' to help or take one of these horses to go get help. At this point we're not that far from Carson City."

There continued to be a lot of back and forth between the men as Ricardo's men waited patiently. The plan formed when Mr. Pritchett gave one of the horses to the older Wells Fargo man to go for help.

"I figure these other two young know-it-alls might be better help than you anyways." He grinned. "We'll get started, while you go get help. Get back here soon as you can. This coach loaded with so much gold needs that horse."

When he disappeared down the road, the others began to move rocks by hand or rolling them with as much determination as a dung beetle.

Two Pulls nodded to Ricardo and slipped away to intercept the rider before he reached Carson City. He knew without a saddle and carrying the reins in one hand, a shotgun in the other, the Wells Fargo man wouldn't be able to let the animal go with any amount of speed. Two Pulls knew exactly where to intercept him without being spotted.

All the while, the marauders waited.

The sun wore on them as the hours passed and their canteens emptied. One man always stood guard and every twenty minutes switched places with one of the others. Even then it didn't look like much progress had been made. They stopped to wipe their brows when the crack of a twig alerted them. Before they could grab their weapons, a shot rang out, causing the horses to spook and move the coach so the men's attention momentarily diverted. It was long enough for Ricardo to shoot the Wells Fargo man holding the shotgun in the arm. The others were ordered to drop their guns, and when they didn't, one more man took a bullet to the leg.

"I do not want to kill you," Ricardo announced, careful to use an Indian accent.

The men were too exhausted by now to put up any arguments and seemed to realize they had been tricked into working themselves into a weakened state. They were soon tied to trees and given drinks of water. The marauders took their time in taking the gold dust and coins from the strong box.

Unbeknownst to the marauders, the Washoe Indian had been ambushed by the very man he hunted. Because of that one change in plans, the sheriff and posse of Carson City were soon hot on the trail of Ricardo Sanchez and his marauders. Within three days' time they were pinned down with, what seemed to be an unending supply of bullets. Only Sanchez survived along with the secret of where he'd buried the gold.

Even after days of brutal interrogation, Sanchez never revealed where he'd buried the gold. He was soon tried and sentenced to twenty years in prison. He took amusement in looking out his cell window and bragged to the guards he could see where he buried the gold in the distance. After just eight years, he was released to return to a normal life. An orphaned red-haired girl, named Rosie waited for him. Now she had a young son with his dark skin and her blue eyes. When Sanchez died a few months later of pneumonia, Rosie and the child disappeared to Virginia City, investing in land, a general store and a boarding house. She soon became the most powerful and respected woman in the territory.

Speculation was that a wealthy aunt had left her the money because of the child with questionable heritage. Wherever it came from, Rosie never married, saying she didn't need a man to make her happy or pay her way. And she certainly didn't need one to tell her what to do.

When rumors circulated from time to time concerning the Wells Fargo gold that was never found, men would talk around campfires, on barstools or after prayer meetings about searching one more time for such treasure. The flurry of activity in the mountains would soon die out when nothing was discovered.

Only Rosie would listen to their disheartened stories and smile with a sense of victory having risen above it all. No one could explain how such a simple girl grew to be one of the richest and most powerful women in the territory.

MARTYRS NEVER DIE

Secret Service invited the Enigma Team to be seated to view the security footage from the night before. They all looked exhausted after the nearly failed attempt to protect the crown prince of Saudi Arabia. One agent was missing and the Enigma leader said she was resting.

"Let's get started. We can have a face to face with her when this is done if need be. She was banged up and bloody. Don't blame her for sleeping in. We've secured the prince."

Agent Evans, the lead with Secret Service, walked by them and nodded to the chairs around the table. "Last night you spoke about this woman like she's a cupcake." His grin was a little unsettling. "Pay close attention to the video and learn." He called for the rest to be seated and then spun his finger in the air toward someone sitting at a computer. "I want her with Secret Service."

The security footage filled the screen in the front of the room.

~ ~ ~ ~

Tessa pulled free of the prince's unexpected embrace and eased in front of him, when an intruder entered the suite. Where was her purse with her weapon? Wasn't that the man the prince claimed to be his assistant? He looked a little rough around the edges to be in such an important position.

"Stop right there. How did you get in here?" Where was her backup? She tapped her earwig. "Assistance needed." Nothing. She held up her hands to look threatening.

"It's just Amir," the prince sighed, as he stepped around Tessa.

Amir was only about five foot eight. In spite of wearing a long white tunic and a draped keffiyeh that fell to his shoulders, Tessa noticed he was slender and wiry. Dark circles surrounded his eyes, the color of obsidian, adding an almost mystical vibe to his long narrow face that resembled chiseled granite. The loathing in his eyes as they slid up and down her body, chilled her to the bone. Was this a test of her ability to be a good field agent?

Tessa threw her arm out to stop the prince. "I said stop, Mr. Amir. Now you step back and hold out your arms until I can search you." He raised his arms as she approached and noticed the look of evil in his eyes. She didn't like it. His fingers twitched, and he batted his eyelids one too many times. Watching all those westerns with her dad told her this character was about to draw his gun.

When she stopped three feet from him and locked gazes, she heard the prince laugh. "Honestly,

Tessa. It's fine. I'm sure your people let him in."

"No. They didn't. Did they, Amir?"

"Don't be a martyr, woman."

One corner of his mouth turned up in a smirk as his eyes narrowed and he dropped his arms, then lunged at her. He spun her around and held her with his arm around her neck and pulled her tighter up against his body. Reaching into his tunic, Amir pulled out a gun and pointed it at the prince.

A bewildered expression flooded the prince's eyes as his forehead creased in unbelief. He took a step forward, causing Amir to jab the weapon into Tessa's temple. "Amir," he snapped. "What are you doing? She is a friend. I will have your head for this," he fumed. "Release her immediately."

"I don't take orders from you, Your Royal High and Mighty. You will never live long enough to hurt me or anyone else in the kingdom. You are finished. My friends and I will see to that."

Four more men in black suits walked through the double doors. Tessa screamed, "run," at the top of her lungs as she jerked her body to the side, catching Amir off guard. At the same time, she doubled her fist and slammed it backwards, with as much force as possible, into his crotch, causing him to release her and bend over with a howl of pain. While he was bent over, she pivoted and clasped her hands together in a fist, then pounded it into the back of his neck. On his way down to smash his face into the hard tiled floors, his gun flew up into the air.

Tessa caught the gun in midair and glanced over her shoulder one more time. "Now, Muhammed!"

In the next second as the four imposters rushed forward. She fired the gun into the groin of one man in case he was wearing a bullet proof vest. His howl echoed through the room as he tumbled to the floor, trying to cover the pool of blood forming on the front of his pants.

In that same split second, one man helped Amir up off the floor and heard him say, "He's getting away. Kill the woman. Now."

She was faintly aware Amir and the man were now free to attack the prince. The second man, left to finish her off, let out a yell that forced Tessa to stumble back against the couch. She fired once and missed. She pulled the trigger again, only to have it jam. With the aim of a St. Louis Cardinal pitcher, she hurled the weapon at his face, making contact. He stumbled backward for a moment and shook his bulbous head as if dazed.

She slipped around the couch as he continued to approach with outstretched arms like a grizzly bear. When he reached inside his suit jacket, she assumed it was for a gun, but he withdrew a knife that looked like something from a horror movie and could easily take out a room full of zombies.

The only thing to do was something he wouldn't expect. She hiked up her dress to the top of her thighs, which in itself caused him to pause. Then with a hop onto the coffee table, she grabbed up some marble chess pieces and threw them at him, giving her enough time to leap onto the sofa. The springs gave her enough bounce to land on the back. Before the man could react, she pulled out the chopsticks holding her hair in a bun, one in each hand and lunged toward him, jamming them into his unprotected eyes. One went in and the other snapped in two, but left a large gash in his cheek.

He howled liked a wounded animal then staggered backwards, dropping the knife at the same time. Tessa grabbed the knife and buried it once in each thigh. She didn't know if she'd hit an artery or not, but blood sprayed over her bare legs and arms as she straightened to pivot toward the missing prince. Two down. She doubted this one could walk or even see where he was going, so finishing him off needed to wait.

The sound of breaking glass and guttural noises came from the kitchen-game room. Grabbing her discarded Stilettos off the floor, she ran into the room to find both Amir and another man closing in on the prince. To his credit, Prince Muhammed was fearless as he held up a pool stick and swiped it at Amir, making contact enough to cause the second man to dodge as it struck his shoulder. The intruder managed to grab the narrow end and tried to pull it away from the prince with no success. Then suddenly the prince released it, causing the second man to fall off balance.

Without hesitation, Tessa aimed the high heel at the base of his skull, burying it enough to draw blood and drop him to the floor. With a glance toward the prince who was trying to finish Amir, she used everything in her power to jump on the back of the attacker. He spun around and grabbed her by the forearms. By using his grip on her against him, she jerked the back of his hand, knuckles out, to slam into his other arm, which hurts like the devil. Her brutal training had finally come in handy.

As his grip released, he stepped back only to have Tessa go after him and slip a hand in his suit coat. With her thumb, she jammed it into his chest above his left breast. It should've felt like he was having a heart attack. Either way he sucked in his breath and leaned toward her as if he would fall forward. Tessa took advantage of the moment of confusion to snatch up the pool stick he dropped on the floor. As he looked up in pain, Tessa slammed the wood into his nose so hard it shattered. At least he was no longer a threat.

Now her attention was completely on the prince. Amir took one of the pool balls and threw it at the prince, who took it on the chest. She spotted her purse and snatched it up, only to find her Kyber was gone. Amir turned his attention to her now and started throwing pool balls at her. Four hit her in various places, causing a burst of pain. If his aim had been better, she realized she'd be dead of a head injury.

The last one he hurled at her, she caught in midair. She needed to remember to thank her dad for making her play baseball with her brothers. She was one heck of a second baseman and later, a pitcher in high school.

"Looking for this?" Amir smirked as he pointed the gun at her.

The prince picked up an eight ball he'd grabbed off the floor and propelled it at Amir. The keffiyeh rope around his head took the brunt of the blow but caused him to drop the gun and turn back toward his intended target. The prince grabbed a carving knife from a knife block set on the counter and rushed toward Amir.

Although the prince seemed to be getting the best of Amir, he managed to get free without harm. He took two steps back when Tessa secured the gun and fired. Unfortunately, she missed as he turned and ran for the outside. Both she and Prince Muhammed chased after him. Tessa fired again when he fell into the pool. The prince jumped in after him but couldn't keep up.

Before Tessa could circle the pool, she watched Amir climb out and run to a closed bench. Opening it, he jerked something out and slipped his arms through it. He climbed onto the ledge and smirked at her, then pointed toward the pool. When she started after him, she glanced toward the prince still in the water just as Amir stepped off the edge into the night.

Where was he? Then she saw him struggling and went beneath the water. Without another thought, Tessa jumped in and caught him around the neck as he seemed to lose consciousness. She managed to pull him to a platform barely rising out of the water then higher where it was dry. He wasn't breathing.

"Come on. Come on," she coaxed as she performed CPR. As she rolled him to his side, he spit out water and started to cough. When he smiled up at her, Tessa could only feel a wave of relief and pulled him up into her arms. "You'll live. You okay?"

"Maybe you should hold on to me a minute to make sure," he smiled.

Tessa laughed then noticed the man she'd broken a pool stick across his nose, had staggered out to the pool. "I need to finish something. Wait here."

When the man saw her rise from the platform, he pooched out his bloody lips and motioned for her to come at him. Tessa slowly approached and realized she may have gotten too close when he doubled his fist and took a swing at her head. But her training once again kicked in and she used her elbow to plow into his upper arm, which caused a sharp pain to vibrate down to his fingertips.

Before he gained control, she slammed the palms of her hands against his ears. A moan of pain escaped his mouth as he bent over only to meet Tessa's knee under his chin, forcing him to bite his tongue. He then spit out a few teeth and hit face first onto the pool deck.

The sound of banging on the suite doors reached her as she helped Prince Muhammed to his feet. "I think help has arrived, Prince Muhammed. You'll be safe now."

The prince surveyed the area as they moved toward the living room. "Safe? What do you call all this? Who needs them?"

Tessa picked up a knife from the floor, just in case, as the front doors burst open. There stood the Enigma Team, staring at her like she'd sprouted a forked tail and horns. She tried to smile, but her face hurt. "I was just going to call you."

Prince Muhammed leaned into her body, smeared with pool water and blood, then offered a weak smile to the surprised rescue team. "Can I keep her?"

She chuckled as they both limped into the room, enjoying the look of shock on the faces of men who thought she was only good for gathering intel.

~ ~ ~ ~

The lights brightened the room as the security footage ended. "I don't know who this woman is or why I haven't heard about her before, but she has single handedly saved us from an international incident." Agent Evans frowned at the Enigma Team and his own Secret Service agents. "The rest of you morons can expect a paid vacation to Quantico for a little refresher course." He pointed to the computer tech. "Let's watch that security footage one more time. Popcorn anyone?"

THE RED DOT WAR:

The Landing of Commander Rook

The air on Earth took some getting used to but it was manageable. It wasn't as clean as his home, but then again it hadn't been home for some time. With the rescue operation completed, he made the difficult decision to step into his new role as a normal human on this planet. Part of him felt exhilaration at the prospect of the exploration and discovery. The other part dreaded the confusion at the incompetence of a species he really had never understood, even after studying them when the idea of escape had materialized.

What was done—was done.

His lead team was already at work here in the United States and others had been freed in locations throughout the world according to their interests, abilities and expertise. With any luck they would not be discovered. The Americans were another matter. They had an overabundance of interests in all things UFOs, aliens and something called Star

Wars. That could prove to be problematic if The Clans came looking for the escapees. It was his hope by then they would have assimilated enough to remain invisible to their boorish ways.

And they would come. There was too much at stake to let them wander about the galaxy unsupervised with the vast amount of knowledge and capabilities at their disposal. The Clans were insanely jealous of this power and intended to stomp it out before he led his teams to victory. For now, he would concentrate on information recon, finding a suitable mate and preparing for the coming war, whether that was in a week or ten years.

To fit in, he felt it imperative to find a woman as soon as possible. He wasn't sure exactly what that would feel like here. On his home planet, that part was done for you. There they called it an arranged marriage but frowned upon this in the Western culture of Earth. In his world, some couples eventually fell into a mutual respect and appreciation for one another. It was necessary for population growth. When the Clans took over, many children were removed from homes if they showed promise in certain areas. Because of this the women began to lose interest in having children. The pain was too great and they became sterile. The family unit, although already weak, became impossible to survive.

Before he landed, Commander Rook studied the news releases in the area he hoped to call home. One city had a gathering of sorts, consisting of all manner of creatures and misfits he'd studied the last few years. Some of these characters had become very popular, or so he understood from the statistics. These individuals moved about the country to perform and get their pictures taken at these conventions. He checked his wrist computer again to reassure himself the name was correct. Wizards of Comic Con. He rolled his eyes in impatience. This was yet one more thing he didn't understand about these Earth humans.

Perhaps he'd find like-minded people there to help him with this transition. The belch of car and truck exhaust annoyed him. Not only was it offensive to his senses, but it distracted him from focusing on the plan.

Enter.

Evaluate available intel and participants.

Avoid anyone who may be connected to Clan members.

Don't draw attention to himself.

Catching a glimpse of his reflection in the mirrored windows surrounding the convention center, he guessed blending in would be the easiest part of his reconnaissance. His silver helmet completely covered his head, leaving slits for his eyes and nose. The padded top of his uniform had thin steel shoulder pads that matched the bands that covered the lower part of his arms. Earth humans might mistake his outer shield akin to a bullet proof vest, but it was so much more during confrontation with an enemy. His ammo belt, draped over one shoulder to the bottom of his metal plating might look like a toy, but it was anything but. With his thighs covered in the same bullet-proof armor shield, and the brown belts around the top of his black boots, Commander Rook believed he blended in enough to be invisible to the thousands of people who appeared to be a mix of weird and wonderful aliens, superheroes and monsters.

Why did Earth humans do this?

Someone touched the weapon strapped on his back that resembled a cross between a tuning fork and a narrow crutch. With one swipe, he could easily take down a room full of these bazaar humans. He pivoted and glared at the young boy.

"Sorry." He grinned revealing a missing tooth. "Your costume is so cool." He held up what he imagined was what they call a cell phone. "Can I take a picture of you?"

"No." The commander pivoted and walked away.

He stood in line at a gate where people handed someone a slice of paper then proceeded inside. When it was his turn, the man extended his hand.

"I need your ticket, buddy," he said with such boredom, the commander felt like slapping him upside the head for not taking his job seriously. "Come on, I don't have all day."

The commander waved his hand as if batting a pesky fly. "Let me pass. I don't need a ticket."

"Ha. Great. Another guy who thinks he's Obi-Wan Kenobi. Sorry, hotshot. No ticket. No geek-out adventure for you. Now go over there and get a ticket or I'm calling security. And I mean the real badass guys. Not you."

"Here's a ticket," came a feminine voice. "Got an extra. Won it in a contest. Couldn't get anyone to go with me. Enjoy," she said, handing both tickets to the man when the commander stood there appraising this new human.

"Thank you," he finally said, as she pushed passed him and disappeared into the crowd.

"Well, go on. You're holding up the line," the ticket guy complained.

The convention hall opened up to a display of cosmic lights, unfamiliar spaceships hanging from the ceiling, vendors with everything from swords made with a relic-like machine called a 3D printer, toys, books and science gadgets. Every cubicle and table sold something unique. Posters, costumes, comic books, and knick-knacks appeared to be in great demand by the number of people gathered at the booths.

But it was the people who fascinated him the most. A purple woman with three breasts covered in leather, an overweight wizard who wore a large, pointed hat with a moon on his cloak, a robot character in white with a matching helmet carried a weapon that would do him no good, all stopped in front of the commander and eyed him from head to toe.

"Let me see your identification."

Commander Rook noticed a picture of the exact character on a nearby vendor's wall. He was what the movies called a stormtrooper.

"Go to hell," he mumbled.

The character laughed and kept moving. Apparently, this was supposed to be fun.

It wasn't.

Several people asked if they could have their picture taken with him. He refused and kept walking. Even when two young women dressed in some kind of provocative clothing stopped him and dared touch him, in spite of being tempted, he refused. Taking his picture in this strange land could be trouble. Perhaps coming to this event wasn't a good idea, but the computer had insisted this was where he needed to go in order to find a willing assistant. There appeared to be thousands at this event. Why, he wondered? But he continued to search for the one, taking his time to stop and look at merchandise, listen to promotional nonsense about scientific gadgets that would enhance their geek experience. All the while he'd study the participants, both behind the vendor tables and around him.

Then he felt her for the first time. It was as if someone had jabbed a feathery spear into his heart then withdrew it. He took several steps out into the middle of a wide aisle and realized he was a head taller than most everyone there. Inspecting the crowd, coming and going, he felt her eyes exploring his body. It was not unpleasant. This was not the time to find a mate. The assistant was vital to his smooth transition to this place. A mate could complicate things if she didn't understand why he was here or who he was.

Would she possess the sign of readiness like on his planet? If not, how would he know she was the one who would take his heart and bare him children? He'd read Western women liked to do their own choosing, and many today reserved the right to forego having children in order to have a career. That probably wasn't going to work for him. Yet he couldn't deny the feeling she watched him from a veil of secrecy.

"Skye," a male voice yelled above the noise.

The sudden male intervention drew his attention toward a vendor at the end of the long aisle. He touched the side of his helmet to zero in on the disturbance. Commander Rook slowly turned his head toward the young woman who had given him the entrance ticket. He'd barely looked at her as she tucked it in his ammo belt strapped across his chest, disappeared through the gate and then the crowd. Yet now he noticed. He could feel his mouth tighten into a straight line and his nostrils flare in anticipation.

The male with the loud voice stepped in front of the woman, cutting off his inspection, but she shyly peeked around him as he talked, pointed at the vendor stall, then quickly left. She stared at him again for several seconds until he stepped in her direction. With a clumsy misstep, she escaped behind the table where she turned her back on him. Her attention now went to several 3D printers. She began feeding in information, and they chugged to attention to create an order for, what he imaged was an event participant.

His approach slowed, taking in the environment in all directions, as he often did before charging into battle. Finally, he stopped far enough away he could observe the woman without interruption. Tapping his wrist band, he cloaked his body so as not to be disturbed as he tried to find reason in this matter.

The woman intrigued him with her black leather halter top and a black ballet skirt that protruded outward and resembled a round slice of pineapple. The black fishnet stockings revealed slim legs. Her arms were partially covered in tattoos from her elbows to her fingertips. All manner of colors twisting throughout the designs made him want to smile. Her red hair was pulled up in pigtails, giving her an almost childlike appearance, but the bright red lipstick dispelled that notion pretty quickly when she appeared to be searching the crowd again for him.

She looked right at him, as if she could see through his invisible cloak. The ice blue of her eyes startled him. He'd never seen anything so beautiful. No one on his planet had blue eyes. What caused this mutation? Was it healthy? No matter. If she were the one, he would ask her to change them. Maybe.

A customer stepped up and her mouth turned into a wide smile that almost made him lose control of his cloaking device. A malfunction seemed to be affecting his heart, he noticed. It was beating too fast. He slowed it. His clothes were starting to feel tight as he watched her hand the customer some kind of sword made from the 3D printer.

With her being busy again, Commander Rook lost track of the time as he stared and studied this American woman. Every time someone walked away, she searched the crowd. Was she trying to find him? Watching her was not an unpleasant experience like many of the Earth women he'd come in contact with on short trips.

This one did not smell like the others. It was told that your future mate would have a fragrance only you could detect. With sensory overload in such a large complex and thousands of people, he found it odd that he could separate everyone into one category and this creature into one all by herself. Once more he began to focus on the tattoos down her arms from her shoulders beneath the lacy fishnet that clung tightly around her skin.

He lied to himself thinking it was only a curiosity about whether the tattoos might be a hidden language. The overpowering urge to touch her fingers dancing across her tablet keys when someone paid for a product, both surprised and irritated him. He felt as if he was losing control because of this ridiculous sensation running up and down his body.

It was not entirely unpleasant. He wasn't sure of the protocol moving forward. Women had interested him in the past, but it had been only in a plutonic relationship for the most part. From what he had read, a sexual relationship on this planet involved different concepts of interaction. This seemed a little unorganized to him if not messy and time consuming.

The man giving her directions earlier returned and joined her in the booth. Was this her father? The distance in age felt appropriate. He handed her a cup of something which she immediately sipped then smiled. He noted the smell for future reference as well as the man sharing in the activity. Apparently, these humans shared a kind of friendship over this gesture. Noted.

Once more, she gazed around the area, searching, but for what or who? Then she stared right at him. He checked his invisible cloak and felt confident he remained secure. Yet, her penetrating gaze began to eat away his ability to hold tight the wrap around him. When she tilted her head and took one more sip of the brew, she then smiled right at him, sending shock waves through his body. The cloak retracted and he stood visible and vulnerable to the masses.

The sudden appearance caused her to jerk her drink enough that it splashed onto the table below. Slowly, she lifted her wide eyes back to him, transfixed, as was he. Her red lips parted slightly as if she wanted to speak, but couldn't. Strangely, he understood this new sensation.

"Hello," another male groaned at her. "I'm waiting for some service." Two more young males joined the rude intruder and smirked. They were all dressed in some kind of fake military uniform.

The woman continued to stare at him without acknowledging the customer.

When he snapped his fingers in front of her eyes, she blinked and stepped back so that her boss stepped forward.

"I can help you. Do you have an order?" He gently pushed the woman away from the table and mouthed to her, "It's okay."

The customer produced some kind of dagger from a bag and dropped it on the table. "I ordered this from you, and when I got it in the mail it was cracked. I want a refund."

"Of course. Do you have your receipt or shipping information? I can trace it." He picked up the tablet.

"No. It's got your name right here." He pointed to something on the hilt of the reproduction.

The vendor took it and adjusted his glasses. "This was discontinued two years ago. Where did you get this?"

"I ordered it from you."

"I'm sorry. We don't sell these anymore. Maybe you got it from a third-party vendor." He handed it back. "I can't help you unless you have a paper trail."

The customer reached across the table, grabbing the man by the front of his wizard outfit, and jerked him forward. "Give me back the money or I'll tell everyone who walks by what a liar and a thief you are."

The girl tried to pull the man back then slapped at the customer's hands. All three of them laughed as he was released. Now he reached for her and caught her arm.

"Aren't you a pretty thing. What are you supposed to be? Some kind of Anime cartoon?" She tried to free his grip. "Tell you what. Let's go get acquainted and we'll call it even."

Commander Rook stepped forward and touched the man's shoulder, applying pressure with his finger so hard it felt like an electrical shock. He jumped back with a howl. His two friends appeared startled for a few seconds then took on a rigid fighting stance.

"You need to leave now." The commander realized it sounded like an order. By the head-to-toe appraisals they were giving him, he guessed they were trying to decide if they should make a scene. He remained quiet and continued to glare at them. Since they couldn't see his eyes or speculate on his body language, they began to back up.

"This isn't over," warned the aggressive one.

"Yes. It is. If I hear one disparaging word about these people, I will come looking for you." When the customer narrowed his eyes and doubled his fists, the commander reached out and snatched him up by the collar and held him a foot off the ground with one hand. "Repeat after me." He gave a small shake as the man grabbed at the commander's grip. "I apologize for being an inconsiderate idiot." The commander slid his free hand up to his throat. "I'm assuming you are unable to speak in your current situation. I'm going to let you down and motivate you to speak. Understand?" He nodded the best he could. "Very well."

Commander Rook pivoted toward the table and the stunned vendors. He dropped him, causing him to fall forward across the table.

"He has something to say."

"I apologize," he began to stutter, "for being an inconsiderate idiot."

The commander slapped him on the back and then made a circular motion before jerking him back upright. "Well done. Now, you and your," he eyed the other two who had turned ashen, "followers should move along, before you get into any more trouble."

With a final shove, the man crashed into the other two, making them look like clowns. They slinked off like embarrassed schoolboys as the surrounding vendors and customers began to applaud the commander. He didn't understand the attention, but it felt like he'd made an impression.

He turned back to find the girl gone.

"Where is she?" He couldn't help sounding like the authoritative commander that was his life.

The older man pointed toward a crowd of people standing in line for autographs from someone with pointed ears and a weird haircut. There was, what humans call a movie, running behind him, where he stood on the bridge of a spaceship with others dressed in the same kind of uniform. One more thing he did not understand. He pivoted to leave when the older man reached out and touched his forearm. The commander gazed down at the hand and removed it carefully.

"Skye is different. She's not like other girls. Don't take offense if she won't speak to you. It's hard for her to communicate sometimes."

The commander nodded. "Noted. I mean her no harm."

Skye appeared to wait patiently until it was her turn for the autograph. The character invited her to have her picture taken with him, and she offered a shy smile and obliged by handing someone her phone. Mr. Pointed Ears wrote something extra down on the autograph. Whatever it was surprised her as she looked back at him and blinked rapidly. She stared at the note without watching where she was headed, plowing into him. If he hadn't reached out for her, Skye would have ended in an undignified sprawl on the floor.

"Oh," she whispered. "I'm. Sorry." She clung to the autograph with both hands. "You are the one who helped us at the table."

"Yes." He wondered why his voice now sounded so robotic to him. "May I see your paper?" He took it before she gave him permission, but didn't resist. The character with the pointed ears had added a series of numbers. "What are these numbers? A code?"

"I think it's his cell phone number."

"Code for see you later?" he asked in disgust. "He is up to no good. You must come with me."

~ ~ ~ ~

"I am in need of an assistant." She continued to stare at him wide-eyed and mute. She'd grabbed the paper given to her by the pointed eared man out of his hand. Now she gazed at him with those penetrating blue eyes. Witchcraft was his first thought before he ran a search on his helmet computer. Apparently, many humans on Earth had this trait and wasn't because of any defect or magical mistakes caused by those called Thornes on his planet. "I repeat. I am in need of an assistant. I have chosen you."

His last words caused her to tilt her head and examine him from head to toe. Once more there was a tightening of his clothing and a warm sensation that spread throughout his body. On his planet, this did not happen to someone like him. He was above being swayed by women and took his pleasure whenever the need arose. It had always been a mutual experience and he rarely gave the practice another thought once finished. For reasons unknown to him, Rook found it puzzling that he actually wanted to impress this human.

When she reached out timidly and touched his armor, he decided letting her run her hand up and down his arm, then walking around him, touching him here and there, was a bit mind-bending. The biggest surprise was he wanted her to keep doing it. Except, he felt there was something off about the young woman, and this also concerned him.

"Follow me. I will talk to the man working your table." She shrugged and strolled casually behind him, stopping several times to look at merchandise in a booth or listen to a sales pitch. She didn't seem to understand the urgency of his need to conclude this process so they could return to his ship.

To add to the sense of chaos he felt, she generated a lot of attention. Attention he really didn't need. They pointed at her then at him like they were a couple. She was clueless. What did her father-figure mean when he said she was special? Was that another way of saying she was simple minded? Perhaps he had rushed to judgement because of the blue eyes and her ability to see through his cloak? Maybe it was her electric energy she transmitted through those long fingers and speckled nails.

He decided to rethink the magic angle.

"Absolutely not," the older man fumed when he suggested she become his assistant. "I'm her guardian and where she goes, I go."

"Very well. You may come. Do you have skills

besides making toys?" He nodded toward their booth.

"They're not toys. We refer to them as collector items."

"I stand corrected. I will stand guard while you prepare to leave."

"Leave? This is how I make my money. I paid four hundred dollars to have this booth. I'm not going anywhere and neither is Skye."

Skye stepped forward and leaned over their display table toward the guardian. "He is the one I told you would come. You must listen to him. I will go with him to do what needs to be done to protect our planet. He is only one, but there are others."

"How do you know this?" Commander Rook asked in amazement.

"The night sky reveals things that no one notices but me. I don't understand it myself. My computer picks up transmissions from your home. I know you are in trouble and need my help."

"I came to make a new life, but others are looking for me."

"I know. I can help you transform to one of us and hide you. Where are the others?"

Commander Rook thought for an instant that she might be play-acting like some of the other characters around the convention center. They pretended to be monsters and aliens he did not know existed. Had she slipped into such a role?

"The others are at different locations throughout your country. We need to work together to prevent our enemy's takeover." He paused and eyed her in bewilderment. "This man says you are special.

What does 'special' mean here?"

"Don't answer that, Skye. If you really want to go, I can't stop you. I knew this day would come. Please. I love you like my own child."

She cocked her head robot-like and reached out her hand to him. "We will come back for you. Do not worry about me." She placed his hand on her cheek. "Thank you, for the life you gave me."

The fatherly figure turned back to the commander. "When I said she was special I'm assuming you are very much like her. She came from—far away and you will soon discover this. I knew this day would come and your people would come for her."

"I do not understand your words," he said, looking between the girl and her father-figure. "No harm will come to her. If she desires for you to join us, I will make preparations for one more."

"I would very much like to be a part of what is about to happen." He then smiled at the girl. "You know how to reach me. I'll be ready."

She kissed his hand and something wet rolled down her cheek.

"Why are your eyes leaking?" he asked, concerned she might be defective.

"We should go now," she said, taking his hand. "I will help you."

The commander and the strange girl in the tutu meandered through the many aisles of the bazaar booths and characters until they exited the building. She skipped once outside and twirled around like she'd been set free from an inner demon. When a happy sound came from her mouth, Rook froze and stared at her.

"I've never heard this sound."

"It's called laughter. Sounds of joy."

"I thought it was what you Earth humans call music."

"I suppose in a way it is."

"I feel pleasure when you do this." He began to walk again and she followed, pointing out various things along the way that had puzzled him earlier. It bewildered him, once more, how she knew that he wanted to know these things. The red dot on her forehead glowed now and he had no hesitation in claiming her for his own.

The world was about to make sense for him and he sensed something miraculous was about to fill his new life. This girl, no, this woman, was the one he'd searched for his entire life. How she'd ended up on Earth was a piece of the puzzle yet to be discovered. Even when they reached his ship, cloaked among the forest, she showed no surprise or trepidation. With wonder in her eyes, she followed him aboard and into the life destiny held for her.

UNDER THE SAHARA MOON

They had floated from the sky wearing a tandem parachute when forced out of their highjacked plane over the Sahara Desert. Only the flapping of an open parachute, fighting to be reined in, competed with the grunts of Father Mikhail who struggled to wad it into some kind of ball. Petra rushed to assist, and together they managed to get the rainbow fabric under control. They placed it on the burning sand to use as a seat.

It occurred to her this new partner remained a mystery. He had appeared at her museum with the good wishes of her boss, then found herself on a plane with the man who claimed to be a Greek Orthodox priest. She didn't believe someone who drove a motorcycle like a bat of Hell, wore leather and boots, sported tattoos on his neck and arms, was a priest. With that shaggy hair and blue eyes, he could have passed for a bad boy rockstar with a mug shot. But he held the key to getting her into the treasured structures of Lalibela. That was why she agreed to this partnership.

"Where do you think we are?" asked Father Mikhail.

Feeling beads of sweat drip into her eyes, Petra surveyed the area around her. The cell phone she secured in her pocket, pinpointed their location on the GPS map, but revealed emptiness. Even when she squeezed the map to see a wider version of where they were, nothing popped up.

She shook her head. Who could survive in such a harsh landscape, although she guessed it would be Tuaregs? Without water they would die soon enough.

"Google, where is the nearest water supply?" She had to repeat it three times. "Father, if I were you, I'd say a prayer right now that we make it to this speck on the map or we'll die."

Two hours later an image appeared in the hazy distance. Moving forward became more difficult with each minute. Once Petra fell and Mikhail struggled to pull her to her feet.

"We're almost there. Keep going. Don't give up," he coaxed through parched lips.

Thoughts began to swirl in her head about how she'd gotten here, and she'd probably die without knowing love. The priest trudged onward, but his shoulders sagged with fatigue. He stopped every ten steps or so to let her catch up and finally took her hand to pull her forward.

When he stopped to squint toward the horizon, she wondered if they were lost. She opened her mouth to speak but a wind gust smacked her with enough sand to choke off any words. Mikhail appeared dazed and disoriented as he dropped her hand. He pointed toward the horizon and tried to smile, but it faded as concern creased the lines around his eyes. Petra sunk to her knees. Nothing was left inside her except despair.

Mikhail stumbled to her side then slipped to his knees. Was he praying for her?

Darkness covered her fear of dying as she eased

into some other dimension of survival. She felt her body lift, and the thought of fighting against death, evaporated.

~ ~ ~ ~

The smell of animals and the feel of folds of cloth covering her body, dragged her back to reality. Along with the sound of flapping fabric came murmurs of men's voices. It caused enough confusion to delay her opening her eyes as she tried to piece together her situation. Am I dead?

Something touched her face, then pressed what felt like fingers to her neck.

"Pulse is strong now," came a familiar voice. "Petra?" A damp cloth touched her forehead. "Petra. I need you to drink."

The voice enticed her enough that her eyelids began to flutter. Her tongue ran across her lips at the same moment she realized a person spoke to her. With a sense of fear mixed with relief, she bolted upright to see a man clothed in white, kneeling next to her. His head was wrapped in a dark blue turban that matched his eyes. The lower part of his face was covered, but as she stared at him, he removed it to reveal his identity.

"Petra." Mikhail's wide smile was infectious. "Drink this."

He offered her a cup of water, but it tasted metallic. She gulped the warm liquid. It trickled down her chin which she quickly rescued with a finger and stuck in her mouth. Another man watched her from behind Father Mikhail. Once they made eye contact, he squatted next to the priest as if to get a better look at her.

Dressed in blue robes and a navy turban, she realized they were among the Tuareg of North Africa. He dropped his mouth covering and smiled at her as his eyes ran over her hair. His beautiful light brown face was accented with a thin black mustache. Although his eyes were wide, they appeared hooded and sleepy. With his chiseled cheekbones, he reminded her of a desert bandit created in Hollywood.

"You have hair of fire." He made circles with his finger then elbowed the priest. "Is she your woman?"

"We are…" Mikhail arched an eyebrow and raised his chin, "searching for a friend. We need to find him."

Taking another sip of the strange colored water helped her gather her faculties, when she realized she was dressed in robes too.

"Do you have a husband, Petra?" the man asked. His smile continued as he relieved her of the cup. "A woman in the desert, all alone is not a good thing, especially one that is so beautiful."

Father Mikhail stood up then offered her a hand. "Petra is her own woman. I am merely her spiritual advisor."

Petra flinched at his comment, knowing full well that might mean she'd get a visit from the Tuareg nomad in the middle of the night. Single Tuareg women were free to take multiple lovers until they married. Even after they married, they remained in control of their own possessions. If they chose to divorce, they got to keep their wealth.

Slipping her hand in Mikhail's, she allowed him to tug her up. The Tuareg stood at the same time, never letting his flirtatious smile fade. "I will leave now. Preparations are being made to feed you. Later we will head out to Mano Dayak. There you can continue your journey by plane. My people are anxious to visit, so please," he fanned his hand toward the open flap used as a door, "refresh and join us. I hope you and I can become better acquainted, Petra." His devilish smile widened as he bowed his head.

"Thank you for your kindness..." she didn't know what to call him.

He laid a hand on his heart. "I am Reza Ag Meslar."

There was magic in his charming grin and Petra knew this was exactly the kind of thing that had gotten her into trouble before with men. She was a sucker for fantasy romance and Reza had that written all over him.

"We won't be long, Reza." She couldn't resist a coy smile as she tilted her head at the man who must have saved them.

As he disappeared out the door, Mikhail blocked her view of the Tuareg. His pinched forehead indicated anger.

"Are you flirting with him?"

"Of course not."

"I might be a priest but I know flirting when I see it."

"Are you speaking from experience?" she snapped.

"This isn't downtown USA, Petra. Things are different here. For all I know you just indicated you wanted to have Reza's baby."

"Hmm. That's a pleasant thought," she cooed, as her index finger tapped her cheek. When a look of horror crossed Mikhail's face, she chuckled. "I'm kidding. Relax. Tuareg women are allowed to exert themselves as free thinkers."

"How did you know he was a Tuareg?"

"Duh. I'm a cultural archeologist. He's wearing blue. They're sometimes referred to as the Blue Men. The dye comes off on their faces giving them a sheen. Kind of romantic, don't you think?"

"I wouldn't know." Mikhail's lips puckered in a frown that made his face hard.

"Like hell. Oh sorry. My bad. Like whatever."

"You enjoy taunting me, don't you? I thought with your particular specialty, you would appreciate the spiritual realms of culture."

"Blah. Blah. Blah. You're only trying to put me in my place."

"I seriously doubt you even know your place."

Petra paused and realized everything he'd accused her of was true. "I apologize. I have not always been as polite as I should have been. After all you did put yourself in danger and—"

"Saved your scrawny neck. I could have left you on the plane, or even the desert." Mikhail shook his finger at her.

She opened her mouth to protest but bite her lip instead as she decided looking at him dressed like a Tuareg was a little more attractive than she'd noticed earlier. "Of course, you're right Father

Mikhail." Saying 'Father' in front of his name took the edge off her sudden carnal imagine of him sprawled on a rug next to her under a Sahara moon.

"What?" he fumed. "Why are you looking at me that way?"

~ ~ ~ ~

The Sahara moon loomed over the horizon like a giant white orb. The night air now felt cool against Petra's face as she watched the dancing flames of a small fire. The women had led her outside and found her a place to sit. When Father Mikhail appeared, their attention shifted to him. It wasn't hard to discern from their shy smiles, the goal was to get his attention. If only she could tell them they had a fat chance in Hell making that happen. Besides, he soon disappeared with the man, Reza, she'd met earlier.

Camels lined the edge of the camp with several prepared to travel. The music of a high-pitched horn played as drums beat rhythmically. The trill of the women's tongues lifted, as Petra experienced a thrill at what she was about to witness. Four men dressed in black, marched out before the seated crowd and moved back and forth with the music. Each held a three-foot long stick in their right hand and touched the ground as they swayed. Then the movements switched to their bodies bending and touching the ground.

Petra's heartbeat increased to the beat of the Tuareg magic. The dancers twirled their swords, decorated with fringe and colored ropes. Two split off and began to pretend to be opponents while the twirling and dancing never stopped. Their faces, shrouded in black cloth from the nose down, made Petra wonder how they managed to breath and dance.

When the women began to sing, two more men, dressed in black, emerged from a tent. Burgundy and lime green sashes crisscrossed their chests and wrapped around their waists. Each carried two swords. They began a threatening dance, swinging the weapons and jabbing at each other, making contact from time to time.

The crowd cheered them on as they completed the routine, then the music stopped. The two men bowed to each other. Petra could hear them laugh. It made her feel free from the trappings of civilization.

Both men turned to stare at her as if they could read her mind. The shorter one elbowed the taller of the two and pointed his sword her way. She watched him pull his shoulders back and hand the weapons to his opponent. A shiver touched her spine as he stepped toward her. She made a quick visual search for Mikhail, but he was gone. Did she even care?

The slow, determined steps of the man in black approached her as darkness fell all around them. The crackle of the fire and murmurs of the Tuareg people floated on the cool night air. Then he was in front of her, only his eyes were visible, and even those were squinted in examination. She felt captivated. He lowered his body in a squatting position and removed his mask.

Petra sucked in her breath. "Father Mikhail," she

stammered. The women near her giggled and moved away.

"Petra," he said matter-of-factly. His eyes remained squinted so the blue steel color was invisible. "You have caused quite a stir among the men with your flaming red hair and pale skin. I suggest you choose me right now or you may have a number of interested visitors later. Reza being one of them."

She extended her hand to him. His eyes raked over her face then body. Standing, he took her hand and pulled her up. The nearness was too close, making her aware Mikhail held secrets of his own. If he were a priest then a lot of women at the church were going to Hell with their carnal thoughts.

"Follow me," he ordered.

Petra pulled part of the head covering around her face and followed obediently until they entered their tent. With the head covering dropped, Mikhail removed his turban and loosened the burgundy sashes.

"What?" he asked flippantly. "You knew it was me out there dancing around like an idiot to impress you, right?"

"No. I had no idea," she admitted. "You were trying to impress me?"

"I had to do something the way you were mesmerized by those Tuareg men."

"It was merely a cultural fascination. It's what I do. Or have you forgotten?"

"Well, that cultural fascination could have gotten you a lover if I hadn't stepped in to claim you."

"So, you're my lover for the night?" She cooed.

"You're not my type."

"What is your type, Father Mikhail?" she snapped.

He straightened and raised his chin. "I have pledged myself to God. I have no earthly desire to partner with you or anyone else."

"Partner? Is that what they're calling it in church these days?"

"I resent that you always feel led to tease me. And I certainly don't appreciate your constant flirting with me."

"Flirting with you?" she gasped. "You've got to be kidding." She stormed up to him a little closer than she'd planned. This caused him to stare down at her with those angry blue eyes that nearly made her forget what she'd plan to say. "You are a pompous ass. You know that?"

"Now that I know your type of man, I'll be sure not to display that trait to tempt you." His voice was so unconcerned and cold, it caused Petra to step back and blink with unbelief.

She wasn't used to being stood up to, and when someone tried, she used her womanly charms and tricks to get what she wanted. Father Mikhail infuriated her to the point she couldn't respond to his question.

"Now I get the silent treatment?" He lifted his eyes to Heaven. "Thank you, Jesus."

"I don't know why you're so irritated with me, but we've got to work together to find the treasure. It's a wonder we're not dead after that jump into the desert. Lucky, Reza found us."

Mikhail found a rug and spread it on the ground.

When he sat down, he drew up his knees and eyed her like she was his property. "Luck had nothing to do with it."

"Let me guess. Divine intervention." He patted a space next to him. With a huff of annoyance, she flopped down next to him, aware of his eyes still probing her body, head to toe. "Move over," she said, pointing to the end of the rug. He attempted to scoot, but he still monopolized the area.

"This is more than enough room for both of us to sleep. We need to rest while we can."

"Fine." She laid down then rolled to her side, away from him. "I'll warn you. I'm a bed hog and a very restless sleeper. Give me plenty of room." The rug might have been big enough for two people, but having him so close as she felt him lie down, unnerved her.

Flickering lights from outside, seeped in enough to make patterns dance around the small tent. She hated sleeping on the ground, especially with a self-absorbed priest on her backside. When she noticed his breathing had slowed, Petra rolled over just as Mikhail's eyes opened.

Those blue eyes pierced her usual self-confidence. He had tucked his arm under his head to add an attempt at comfort.

"Do you want me to roll over? I don't mean to make you feel uncomfortable with me."

She was keenly aware of how low and calm his voice had become.

"Ditto, Father Mikhail."

He grinned. "I'll admit it's been a long time since a beautiful woman was in my bed."

"Guess you'll have something to share at the next gospel retreat with the other fine shepherds of the flock."

He pursed his lips and narrowed those eyes that pierced the soul. "I think I'll keep this to myself."

"When was the last time you were with a woman?"

"When was the last time you were with a priest?" he responded immediately.

"Touché. It's none of your business."

"You took the words right out of my mouth." There was no doubt the smile on those firm lips was making fun of her.

Before she could think of a clever retort, Reza rushed in, causing Mikhail to scramble to his feet.

"My friend, Boco Haram is coming. You will not be safe if found. Come. Everything has been prepared."

Even before he finished speaking, Mikhail reached down and pulled Petra to her feet. He grabbed the pack with their precious map to the Lalibela treasure. "Let's go."

As Reza rushed out into the night, Petra took Mikhail's hand and examined it. "These are not the hands of a priest."

"No. I suppose not." He pulled her into his arms. "Maybe we can talk about that after we escape, unless you'd rather stay here with Reza."

They raced their camels across the desert under the Sahara moon where adventure opened the way to undiscovered treasure and unexpected love. Their partnership became a lifetime of unexplored possibilities.

ABOUT THE AUTHOR

Tierney James – Adventure, Thriller & Romantic Suspense Author

Tierney James decided to become a full-time writer after working in education for over thirty years. Besides serving as a Solar System Ambassador for NASA's Jet Propulsion Lab, and attending Space Camp for Educators, Tierney served as a Geo-teacher for National Geographic. Her love of travel and cultures took her on adventures throughout Africa, Asia and Europe. From the Great Wall of China to floating the

Okavango Delta of Botswana, Tierney weaves her unique experiences into the adventures she loves to write. Living on a Native American reservation and in a mining town, fuels the characters in the Enigma and Wind Dancer series. Now with over sixteen books under her belt, Tierney feels there is no stopping her now.

After moving to Oklahoma, the love of teaching continued in her marketing and writing workshops along with the creation of educational materials and children's books. She likes to tell people a little lipstick and danger makes the world go round. http://www.tierneyjames.com

Speaking at conferences, book clubs, school functions, church and community groups are a few of the things Tierney enjoys doing when not writing her next adventure. She also helps beginning writers in their quest to becoming a published author through her workshops and classes. Family, an adopted dog and gardening fill her life with plenty of laughter to share with others.

Tierney has been an Amazon #1 Best Selling author and won numerous awards for her work.

My Social Media Links:

Facebook:
https://www.facebook.com/AuthorTierneyJames/
Facebook Reader Group:
https://www.facebook.com/groups/2430789897157949
Amazon: https://www.amazon.com/Tierney-James/e/B00C1FB19Q
Twitter: https://twitter.com/TierneyJames1
Website: http://www.tierneyjames.com
Pinterest: https://www.pinterest.com/ptierneyjames/
Instagram: www.tierneyjames7

BOOKS BY TIERNEY JAMES

Enigma Series
- An Unlikely Hero
- Winds of Deception
- Rooftop Angels
- Kifaru
- Black Mamba
- The Knight Before Chaos
- Invisible Goodbye

Stand Alone Novels
- Turnback Creek
- The Rescued Heart
- Dance of the Devil's Trill

Wind Dancer Series
- Dark Side of Morning
- Dark Side of Noon

Education
- African Safari

Education for Marketing
- How to Market a Book Someone Besides Your Mother Will Read

Children's Books
- There's a Superhero in the Library
- Zombie Meatloaf
- Mission K9 Rescue

Made in the USA
Columbia, SC
18 April 2022

59127581R00065